A VII KNIGHTS TALE

HUNTER

A Twisted Fairy Tale

WALL STREET JOURNAL & *USA TODAY* BESTSELLING AUTHOR

SAPPHIRE KNIGHT

HUNTER
VII Knights MC

Sapphire Knight
Wall Street Journal & USA Today Bestselling Author

This book is a work of fiction. Any references to real events, real people, and real places are used fictitiously. Other names, characters, places and incidents are products of the Author's imagination and any resemblance to persons, living or dead, actual events, organizations or places is entirely coincidental.

All rights are reserved. This book is intended for the purchaser of this book ONLY. No part of this book may be reproduced or transmitted in any form or by any means, graphic, electronic, or mechanical, including photocopying, recording, taping, or by any information storage retrieval system, without the express written permission of the Author. All songs, song titles and lyrics contained in this book are the property of the respective songwriters and copyright holders.

Warning: This novel includes graphic language and adult situations. It may be offensive to some readers and includes situations that may be hotspots for certain individuals. This book is intended for ages 17 and older due to steamy, sexy, and hotness that will have you jumping your man. This work is fictional. The story is meant to entertain the reader and may not always be completely accurate. Any reproduction of these works without Author Sapphire Knight's written consent is pirating and will be punished to the fullest extent of the law. Stealing this book makes you a thieving prick, and I hope your tits fall off.

This book is fiction.
The guys are over-the-top alphas.
My men and women are nuts.
This isn't real.
Don't steal my shit, I have bills too.
Read for enjoyment.
This isn't your momma's cookbook.
Easily offended people shouldn't read this.
Don't be a dick.

ISBN: 979-8410305877

Editing by Swish Design & Editing
Formatting by Swish Design & Editing
Proofreading by Swish Design & Editing
Cover design by Tall Story
Cover image Copyright 2022

First Edition
Copyright © 2022 Sapphire Knight
All Rights Reserved

DEDICATION

Those of us who love fairy tales
but prefer them a little twisted and a lot spicy.

A VII KNIGHTS TALE

HUNTER

A Twisted Fairy Tale

PROLOGUE

"Well, hello there, snoozing beauty," I tease, wanting to set her mind at ease. She's in a new place with a man she doesn't know. The last thing I need is the chick flipping her shit and screaming my house down.

She blushes, dipping her head to hide her rosy cheeks in her cornflower-colored locks. She must've been warm while sleeping. The pink on them suits her—such a complimentary flush.

"Why snoozing beauty?" she asks with a laugh, and I crack a grin, unable to hold back my fondness of her sweetness. She's kept the remnants of the light blue dress on, the one I found her in, regardless of me offering her some of my clothes. They'd swallow her up, no doubt, but I'd bet she could make anything look proper. I'm a little shocked at her forgoing the new, clean choice, considering hers is in tatters and weaved with some sort of plant. It has to be scratchy and uncomfortable, but you'd never know it by looking at her young face.

"Because you've slept so long since I found you. I was worried and checked on you, but I think your body was overly exhausted and needed the rest."

"I remember being in the woods, and there was someone there with me. Three others, I believe. One of them was busy worrying over keeping me safe, and the next... well, I don't remember anything afterward. It's all so strangely foggy, with everything mixed up like a dream." She frowns, her irises growing worried. Her small hands fist at her sides as she inhales deeply. With an exhale, she releases her grip and takes another step toward me.

My brow wrinkles at her confession, attempting to understand what it could possibly mean, yet I can't. Was she running from something? I found her alone, no others around her. Were they really attempting to keep her safe? And why her?

"I woke up with your mouth on mine..." she trails off as a new flush spreads down her throat.

Christ, she's adorably innocent and has every protective instinct in me rearing to the surface. I lick my lips, imagining her taste on my tongue if I was to sample the perfectly tanned flesh of her neck. She has no idea of the predator in her midst, and it sends a beat of triumph to my inner beast.

"You'd stopped breathing. I was, well, I was worried you'd die," I say plainly, not pausing to consider how my words may affect her. The only thing on my mind at that very moment was making sure she was breathing and moved to safety.

"You were breathing air into me," she states, almost making it sound like a question. Her naiveté is endearing and only entices me further. Everything about this woman screams for me to claim and keep her, but why?

"Yeah, I started CPR. Thankfully, it worked, and you began breathing strongly again. It sounds odd being that we've only just met, but something about losing you sends a strong pang to my chest," I roughly admit and rub the spot above my heart. Pang is an understatement. When I thought she was dying, it felt like my heart was being ripped from my chest. Never have I experienced something so crippling in nature, especially since I don't know the young woman.

I continue, "One of the guys recognized some of your symptoms. You were in the middle of a serious allergic reaction.

Thankfully, he had an EpiPen and let me have it. I was shocked with how quickly it took effect." And grateful because I had no clue what the hell was wrong with her. She's a beautiful enigma, one I want to figure out but probably shouldn't.

"Thank you for whatever you did to help me." She offers a genuine smile. The fairness of her milky flesh and regality of her features are like no other, the only name that suits her is Sleeping Beauty. "What should I call you?"

"Trust me, it was my pleasure. I'm Philip, but my friends call me Hunter. Whatever you prefer." Putting my lips to hers was no difficult feat. I'd gladly do it again to see those enrapturing irises gaze at me full of gratitude. In my opinion, the sooner, the better.

"My name is Aura. Will you tell me about finding me?"

I tip my head, drinking from my strong black coffee laced with a splash of bourbon. I lift my glass and gesture, "Would you like some coffee?"

She shakes her head. "Only to remember."

"All right then. Come sit, and I'll tell you what I know."

CHAPTER 1

HUNTER

"You with me, Hunter?" Viking asks after the others easily pledge their support for his mission.

"Of course," I rebuke. We're brothers, I'll always have their backs when they need me, and this ride is no different. My loyalty is theirs, as is my knife, should they ever require it. My fingers rub over my leather's cut. This MC is my life, and I'd be lost if I didn't have their friendship and support.

"So we're headed to an island," I rehash. "Have you discovered any more information about it yet? Has your mermaid finally found her tongue?"

He shakes his head at my flippant comment about his woman not speaking when he came across her. "There's a bit of dense forest on parts of the island. Keep your wits about you, we don't know what we're stepping into. We'll split up but not too far away from each other so we can get help if needed."

"Sounds like a plan," I easily agree and strap on my long bowie knife. My gun is next, along with my bulletproof vest. I neatly fold my cut, gazing at it fondly before setting it down with a promise to return to it. There's no telling what we'll find, and I don't want anyone to be able to identify me if something unsavory goes down. I have a dark feeling about what we're about to walk into.

Leaving the comfort of the clubhouse, we climb on our motorcycles. The ground vibrates with the thunder of our engines as we head for the docks. We'll be taking a sketchy route out to the island. Before I ride across any sand, I'll be trading my beast for a Jeep that a buddy of mine offered to let me borrow. He's grabbing the other shit I requested as well. When I called to let him know I'd be in the area, he was more than happy to help and more so when I offered to compensate him for it. Being a bounty hunter, I've met many people in random spots, and over the years, some of them have become useful.

The poor woman Viking found, well, she deserves to be avenged—every woman treated poorly deserves her very own savior. We just so happen to wear a leather vest and ride a motorcycle, but it doesn't mean we can't be our wicked version of heroes if needed.

The ride is swift, the club moving with one purpose in mind. *Vengeance.* We'll never allow such evil to exist as long as we're breathing. I lower my kickstand, climbing free from the white beast of a bike. My knife rests heavily against my side and brings a sense of comfort. I like to call it my truth seeker since it hasn't let me down yet.

I quickly grab for anything I may need out of my saddlebags and fix the straps on the bulletproof vest. Once I've checked out the gear in the back of the Jeep and arranged everything how I want it, I hop into the driver's seat. My knife stays on me at all times. I also keep a handgun in the cubby next to the gear shift for easy access and a shotgun resting beside me on the center console. The few other Nomads I normally ride with load up into the Jeep with me, weapons at the ready.

We wait for the signal from Viking, and once he's set, we take off. The ride to the island is sketchy as fuck but doesn't take long, thankfully. Not that I'd back down or anything, I live for this shit—for the hunt.

I veer off toward the right. I won't stray too far from the pack, but this direction has a bigger clearing, and besides, I work better with just a few guys versus a cluster. "Watch our six," I mutter to Charmer, though it's unnecessary. Diablo, Briar, Charmer, and I have worked together long enough, our roles have become more habitual than anything, and we tend to revert to our designated jobs in sketchy situations.

"I'm not seeing anyone on this side, not even a lookout," Briar comments as he stands in the back, holding onto the Jeep with one hand and a pair of binoculars with the other.

"All clear back here," Charmer calls in return.

"Not a fucking thing here either," Diablo notes, wearing a scowl. His lips are always turned down into a brooding frown. "Malevolent is probably seeing more action watching our bikes than we are out here in bum fuck Egypt."

Charmer snickers, Briar remains vigilant, and I snort. I'm not arguing with the guy, he's probably right. We can usually peg a situation quickly. It's probably what makes us so good at being bounty hunters. "I wonder if it's this quiet on Viking's side of the island?" I murmur as the trail grows remarkably tight. We're battered with thick brush reaching for our flesh inside the Jeep's open doors for a time before I call it and stop the Jeep. "Jesus, I wasn't expecting the area to be so dense. It's a goddamn forest! I guess we're on foot from here, boys. Climb out through the top."

"I knew I wore comfortable shoes for a reason." Charmer points to his shiny black boots with one hell of a rubber sole.

"More tennis shoe than boot, fucking pretty boy," Diablo ribs.

"Don't get pissed, big guy, 'cause your boots are shitkickers and squeeze your fat toes. Maybe you should consider my fashion sense next time."

Diablo growls in response, causing us all to chuckle.

"Okay, fuckers, get serious," I order, and we go into stealth mode. You'd never know we were coming unless we wanted you to. We go about exploring quietly. I know they're still around me because we're in tune with each other's sounds. We've spent too many years working together not to be able to sense the other.

"Definitely people around here," Briar mentions after a while. "I'd say under ten, regularly. Maybe five or so. Probably more over time."

I nod, having picked up on similar clues. Charmer and Diablo close in around us, divulging, "There's something over here. A small structure of some kind."

"A house?" I clarify.

Charmer shrugs. "Not sure, it reminded me of an oversized burrow built into the side of a rock. It's camouflaged well… you wouldn't notice it if you were walking by and not paying careful attention."

"Fuck!" Diablo sighs. "There better not be scorpions or some other crawly shit." His big frame shudders, and my lips twitch in amusement. He's a hefty mean fucker, but bugs creep his ass out.

"Go with Charmer and check it out. We'll vet this area to see if there're any others," I tell Diablo, and he heads off in the direction Charmer appeared from.

I nod forward to Briar, and he moves in sync with me. "Check the trees," I order quietly, keeping my gaze pegged around us for people and traps. We move about twenty feet into the thick forest before his strong grip lands on my bicep with a squeeze. Instantly, I halt in my tracks, meeting his gaze. He gestures with a chin lift and points.

There's a small foot and ankle in sight, but the rest of the owner is hidden behind a massive tree and brush. I catalog the foot—it's dainty, probably a woman or young boy. The skin is pale and filthy. I sign, telling him I'm checking it out and to stay put. This is my business, so any upfront risks, I take them before these guys. I figure it's more my responsibility than theirs. Besides, I'd never forgive myself if they were hurt on my watch.

With careful, quiet steps, I creep to the moss-covered tree. I'm standing directly on the opposite side and work to quiet my breathing as well as relax my pounding heartbeat to be able to hear properly. I wait for a second, then another, and again, another. I can't make out any sounds that aren't my own, so I meet Briar's gaze and sign to him that I think the person is dead on the other side.

His gaze widens, but he holds fast, waiting for me to tell him differently. My guys know their willingness to take my directions could mean life or death for any of us, so they trust my orders. Eventually, I chance a look, checking for weapons, and I'm met with creamy skin and tattered clothing. It's a woman, a young one in rags. Her light blue dress is ripped and tied in several places with vines of some sort. I'm guessing to hold it together on her fragile frame.

I make a noise, hoping to startle her into making a move but get no response. "Miss," I whisper and wait. Still nothing. I watch her for the longest time and swear I don't see her chest move. Carefully, I go the rest of the way around and move to touch her. She doesn't look like she's been dead long, her face and throat are littered with red and pink splotches. It's strange. Could it be an island thing that I don't know about? There's no telling what's on the other half of this place. Hopefully, Viking and the others aren't walking into a trap of some sort.

I kneel at her side, my fingers grazing her wrist. It's warm, so I'm right about her not being dead long. I can't catch a heartbeat, so I release her, sitting back to properly take her in. Surely, she can't be dead if she's so red and splotchy. Did she get stung by something that causes this reaction, then her death?

I release a tense breath and move to stand, but there's something about her making me question myself. Perhaps it's her beauty? Her illusion of innocence? Who knows, but it draws me to try again, whatever it is.

This time I reach for her throat, pushing my fingers to her skin with much more force. I calm my breathing, close my eyes, and concentrate.

Shuffling through my thoughts and feelings, I finally weed out the movement coming from her flesh. There *is* a pulse. It's faint, but it is there. Moving on autopilot, I adjust her body until she's lying flat and tilt her head back. I wave Briar over and begin chest compressions. Depending on how long her body fights me, I may need to trade off with him.

While I count in my head, going through my training to save her life, I can't help but take her form in. She's utterly breathtaking. I can only imagine what she must look like in her prime. I wonder what happened to her. There's no telling—out here so far away from society, it could be anything. I push air into her over and over. Anyone else and I'd have given up at this point. My body burns, even though I work out for hours each day, and I find myself growing slack. Silently, I beg for any god or powerful being out there to give her another chance, to allow me to have a moment with her while she's at her most vibrant.

My mouth is on hers when she gasps, taking in my breath, with lids fluttering. I meet her cerulean gaze and carefully lie her head in my lap. I silently watch as she gasps for air, her hands clutch at her throat, and the sight makes my chest ache.

"Breathe. Try not to panic," I offer calmly, not sure what else to do for her.

Was she poisoned?

"Fuck," Briar curses savagely beside me a beat later and digs into his cargo pocket. He thrusts something at me. "Here, use this. I think it's an allergic reaction. Her throat's swollen, so she can't breathe. The splotches are hives."

My brow scrunches, but I do as he directs. I stab the medication into her flesh, and it begins its magic. The woman clutches to me, never breaking my gaze as I watch life blossom inside her once more. She really was dying, and to witness life fill her once more is a miracle I'll never forget as long as I live.

"You're okay," I console. "We're here, and I won't let you die. Not in my arms," I foolishly promise. I don't have that power, but I vow it regardless.

With a soft exhale, she murmurs, "My prince," then she promptly passes out again. This time, she's breathing and owning every piece of my soul.

CHAPTER 2

HUNTER

"We have to get the fuck out of here." I stand with the delicate woman in my arms and turn to Briar. "Who knows if someone tried to kill her. We have to take her with us."

"But what about the others? Viking?"

"Viking has a plan, so they'll be fine. I don't know if anyone is still looking for this woman. I'm not taking the chance of us waiting around and anything else happening to her after she nearly died."

He nods, heading in the direction we came from. I follow behind, moving swiftly but carefully so as not to jolt the beauty in my arms. She's exhausted, yet randomly flutters her lashes, so I know she's still fighting whatever took her under before.

Charmer and Diablo hear us approaching and meet us on the narrow path. Their eyes widen as they notice our newest addition. "We're leaving," I inform them without time for argument, and we hightail it to the Jeep. Charmer and Briar climb into the back seat, and I hand the woman over. They lay her across their laps, one hand securing her to them while the other is heavy with a Glock.

There's no telling what we may come across on our way out, so better safe than sorry.

Diablo's more alert as we reverse, watching everywhere while I concentrate on driving. It's much too tight for me to turn around, so I can only back up, which doesn't exactly work in our favor when we're in a rush to get the fuck out of Dodge. Viking wasn't kidding, this island is riddled with secrets, those of which I can only imagine the true depth of.

"I'm taking her to my place. I can drop you guys off on my way there, but I want to get her to safety before anyone else is aware of her existence."

"What about the Jeep?" Charmer asks as the thick foliage lets up enough for me to swing the vehicle around and finally stop driving in reverse.

I shift gears, briefly meeting his gaze in the rearview mirror. My stare flicks down to take the woman in, and I reply, "I'll call Malevolent and let him know what happened. He'll take care of it."

"Sounds like a plan, brother," Diablo reassures. This is one of the reasons why I ride with these guys—they always have my back with whatever the issue may be. "Has she said anything? Or are we kidnapping a sleeping woman? This has jail time written all over it."

"Nothing," I grumble and pick up speed as we close in on the road leading back to the mainland. I ignore his jail-time comment because I won't allow it to get that far, that much I know for sure.

Briar snorts, knowing what went down back there. "She called him her prince." I catch his suggestive tone, attempting to rile me as my brothers chuckle. I have no doubt in my mind that if we weren't on alert right now, they'd be giving me a truckload of shit about being a dark prince in disguise.

"A smart-ass biker prince who hunts people down for a living, more like it," Charmer adds, causing the guys to laugh more. I hope she's not hearing any of this. I'm not ashamed of my best friends or anything, I am only worried it'd embarrass her, and the last thing I want is for her to be uncomfortable while knocking on death's door.

I obviously didn't think this completely through, taking a random woman with me in the Jeep full of oversized, rough men. She may be terrified when she catches a good look at them, and I don't want that. She needs to relax after whatever she just went through—anyone would after nearly dying.

"What exactly are you planning to do with her?"

I glance at Diablo and sigh. "I haven't thought too far ahead. She was left for dead back there, and I wasn't going to have that on my conscience. Once she's had time to recuperate, I'll get as much information from her as I can. We'll go from there."

He huffs. "More trouble that doesn't belong to you. Always the knight to go running."

My gaze falls to her in the rearview mirror again. I can't seem to get my fill of checking to make sure she's okay. I shrug. I've always had my nose in a bit of trouble, and it's given me the opportunities to help countless people. "I'm a bounty hunter. It's what I do."

"And I'm there with you, brother, but there's no payday on this load. Just a broad destined to get you into a pile of shit. No telling how deep it'll pile up in the end."

Charmer pipes up, "Ouch, that's harsh."

Rather than replying, he quiets and stares out the window. He's a broody fucker, always has been. He never shies away from giving me his opinion, but he's never been one to fill the silence with words either. I appreciate the trait.

Charmer, on the other hand, is his opposite. The brother always has a grin on his face and is known for the wake of ladies always chasing after him. They all want to be his Mrs. Right, but he's yet to find the one he can't live without. Someone will fill those shoes eventually, that much I'm sure of.

Eventually, we make it to the docks where we'd traded our bikes for the Jeep. Malevolent is right where we left him, clad head to toe in black. He's the biker version of the Grim Reaper with an inky mohawk styled sharp enough you'd swear it could cut, and the glare he wears along with it is enough to make any man pause.

"You ugly fuckers are still breathing, so I take it everything went well?" he grumbles, making all of us smile except Diablo. He peeks his head over the back of the topless Jeep to get a decent look at the sleeping woman. "Who's the secret stowaway?"

"We're straight," I reply. "And we don't know."

His brows kick up. "She doesn't speak, either? What happened to this chick?"

Briar shakes his head. "She talks, just been passed out. Hunter saved her life, gave her CPR and an EPI shot."

"No shit?" Malevolent's gaze meets mine.

I nod. "Giving her a chance to recuperate. Bet your ass once she's awake, I'll find out whatever I can."

"She's hot, so, of course, he'd save her," Charmer ribs, and I roll my eyes.

"I'd have saved her whether she was hot or not."

"Yeah, but this is a bonus. Maybe she'll want to repay you for helping her." The guys laugh while I shake my head. I'd probably be joking too if I knew her back story and what she was about, but at the moment, I know absolutely nothing.

"All right," Malevolent grows serious again. "I've taken care of everything like you asked. Beast is sending one of his prospects to grab your bike, then your cut. Don't shoot the guy if you notice someone random on your property... I know how you get with trespassers. He'll ride your wheels to your place, switch out for the Jeep and drop it back off to your buddy." He holds out a bank envelope full of twenties. "Stick this in the console. The prospect will fill up the tank, clean the Jeep, and keep the rest."

"Thanks, brother. I appreciate it." I'm grateful for his help and the heads-up. He's right, I don't like people on my property unannounced and nosing around. It's one of the reasons why I bought land next to a nature preserve and built my place on top of a mountain. Aside from the Nomads who I regularly work with on our bounty-hunting jobs and my other VII Knight MC brothers, civilians are usually smart enough to stay far away.

I say my goodbyes to everyone, making sure I thank them again, and head home. There was no payout today, it was strictly goodwill toward Viking's chapter. I'll have to catch up with him eventually to find out what went down on his end, but for now, there's only one thing on my mind. The sleeping woman in the back seat whose alluring beauty and secrets have my stomach twisting with unanswered questions

I get home and pull the Jeep into the garage. I leave the woman in the Jeep while I go through my house and check everything over. Hunting after people tends to get you put on the top of their shit lists, and you never know when one of them may decide to pop up again for their perverted version of retaliation. I've been lucky so far in the aspect of them not finding me, but eventually, I'm sure that luck will run out. The home security alarm sensors haven't gone off since I've been gone, so at least that's a good sign.

The house is still in the same shape as I left it. I'm generally a tidy guy. I prefer things to be organized, so my place is clean, and the spare room is ready for guests if needed. Not that I have many or frequent visitors. I pull the bed covers back and make my way out to the garage again.

I'm anxious, which is unusual for me. I'm good about keeping a calm head, but not today, it would appear. I want her to wake up and tell me everything about herself. I need to know it all, right down to the tiniest detail. There's something intriguing about her, and it's not the pertinent detail of her nearly dying. I've seen numerous dead people in my lifetime—it's a hazard of the job as well as being affiliated with the MC. I may have an easygoing nature, but I'm a Nomad. I'm not innocent by any means.

Eager to touch her again, I slide my arms underneath her on the back seat. She's small compared to me and lightweight. Lifting her, I pull her close to my chest, carrying her princess style. She stirs, mumbling in her sleep. The only sound coming from me is my breathing along with my thundering heartbeat pounding away in my chest. I swear it's louder than usual, but I know that can't be possible.

What is it about this woman that makes me want to hold her longer than appropriate? Fighting against the instinct to keep her in my arms, I place her on the bed toward the middle. She's not wearing any shoes, and her dress is torn and tattered from the brutality of being stuck on that unforgiving island.

With quick steps, I dip into the master bedroom and riffle through my dresser for the smallest clothes I own. I return with a black VII Knights MC t-shirt, gray boxer shorts, and white tube socks. Random, but hopefully, it'll be comfortable for her to sleep in.

I give her shoulder a gentle shake until she mumbles again.

"I've got you some clean clothes. Put them on and help yourself to the shower when you're ready. No hurry, get as much rest as you need. I'll grab you a glass of water too. You're safe with me, beauty."

She looks like she's been through hell. I hope she realizes nothing will happen to her here, and I'd never allow anyone near her. She must feel some sense of comfort with me to sleep soundlessly like she has. Unless her body's so out of it, she simply can't help it. Although she has a sweet and innocent exterior, I have a feeling this woman is fiercer than her appearance lets on. She'd have to be, to survive for who knows how long she was stuck out there.

"Thank you," she eventually responds with a whisper and turns on her side, facing away from me. Rather than rouse her again, I leave it for now. She's yet to fully open her eyes since I saved her, and I'm probably prolonging her recovery by bothering her.

It was a busy day, and I'm exhausted too. I leave her door open and the guest bathroom light on in case she needs it, then reactivate my house alarm. There's no way she's leaving or anyone showing up for her without me knowing. I still need to download the Jeep and park it in the driveway for whoever Beast's sending to collect it.

Rather than take care of the vehicle immediately, I head for my shower, needing to wash the grime and salty air of the trip off me. Once I'm feeling fresh, I cook a few grilled cheese sandwiches and some tomato soup. I make some extra in case my guest wakes up, but she never does. I swear the silence in the air seems so much louder than usual, knowing she's only down the hall from me.

I pop in to check on her while I'm unloading my various weapons and supplies, but she doesn't stir. It's almost eerie how soundly she slumbers after who knows what she's gone through.

I leave the Jeep in the driveway and reactivate my house alarm. With nothing else to do, I head to my bed, but sleep's the last thing on my mind.

CHAPTER 3

AURA

Waking up and feeling groggy and disoriented, my body aches, my throat is sore and raw, and I feel like a big chunk of time is missing. Peeling my eyes open, I slowly take in my surroundings, and I know without a doubt in my mind I've never been here before. But everything is fuzzy when I try to remember where I came from or where the place should be—it's like the answers are there, but I just can't access them.

Sitting up, I exhale a deep breath and take in my clothes. They're torn and tattered, but something about them seems familiar—I don't know if it's the color or the garments themselves. My fingers lightly slide over the rough material. There're tiny knots all over it, and I finger them fondly, wishing I knew the story behind them. There's more folded at the end of the bed, and I vaguely remember being instructed to put them on. I ignore the instinct that it's what I'm supposed to do and leave the comfort of the bed.

Nothing in the room reminds me of anything, but something tells me it's not mine. The furnishings and decorations are sparse, leaving no clues. My heart thunders in my chest as I head for the door—anything could be waiting for me on the other side. Strangely, no sense of foreboding fills me, only curiosity and a bit of warmth. Outside my room, there's a narrow hall with more doors. There's a small room almost directly across from the one I was sleeping in—it has a large and small washing tub. Getting clean isn't a priority for me at the moment but rather who the mysterious man was that filled my dreams.

I can't help but wonder was he merely a figment of my imagination, someone I dreamed up when I needed him, or was he truly the prince who came to save me? Memories assault me of a man and woman lying in a bed, one of them on either side of me, reading a book. I was young, yet it feels as if it was only yesterday when it happened. More memories laced with fondness assault me when I think of them, and it hits me—they're my parents. This home is wrong, though, and everything seems so much bigger when I remember them.

Quietly, on light feet, I head in the direction of the inviting aroma. My stomach rumbles loudly, and I clench at the area with my hand. When was the last time I ate? If the sharp hunger pangs in my gut are any indication, I'd say it's been a while. It's probably what woke me up in the first place. The closer I get to the smell, the worse my stomach hurts, but I'm too curious to search for food at the moment.

I come across the kitchen first, the smell leading the way whether I want it to or not. A machine on the counter percolates dark liquid into a glass container. There's a bowl of fruit laid out on one of the counters, making my hands fist from the overwhelming desire to take them all and hide them in my clothes. Food this perfect is rarely openly available. I don't know why I know this, but I do. Not letting myself pause, I continue my exploration.

I'm met with a large room filled with windows beyond the kitchen. Outside the house is a beautiful area full of trees and untamed wildlife for as far as the eye can see. There's a long stretch of multi-colored roses and a small iron table with chairs surrounding it. Still nothing familiar, no matter how much I wish it were. It's quiet, and something about the lack of sound brings me comfort rather than the opposite. My gaze remains locked on the soothing scenery as my mind races to come up with answers I don't have.

I remember being home, but where exactly is home? It's certainly not here—this place doesn't look anything like I'm used to. The trees are different, and the flowers and foliage aren't the same. There were others—three women. I can see their faces and feel their warmth in my heart, but details aren't very clear. They're family but not in the same sense as my mother and father.

Fitting these basic pieces together reminds me I haven't seen my parents in a long time. I was a little girl, that much I know for sure. I live in the trees with these other women, but our home isn't like this. The floor is dirt, and we had little to no belongings. We've learned to use nature for everything.

So, it's true, then—I'm far from home.

After I stand there for who knows how long, I spin around and am met with the man from my dreams.

HUNTER

She's startled. It's the first thing I notice when my eyes meet hers. My mind races with something to say to put her at ease with my presence, but what do you say to someone who's back from the brink of death? I go with the opposite of my usual questioning demeanor. "Well, hello there, snoozing beauty," I greet in the friendliest tone I can manage. I have an abundance of questions, but I feel I won't be the only one.

She blushes, dipping her head in an attempt to hide her rosy cheeks in her cornflower-colored locks. She must've been warm while sleeping. The pink on them suits her, such a complimentary flush.

"Why snoozing beauty?" she asks with a laugh, and I crack a grin, unable to hold back my fondness for her. She's kept the light blue dress on, the one I found her in, regardless of me offering her some of my clean, untorn clothes. They'd swallow her up, no doubt, but I'd bet she could make anything look proper.

"Because you slept so long once I found you."

She's finally awake, and what a sight to behold.

The early morning sun's rays pouring in from the wall of windows along the back of the house manages to accent every inch of her. Hard to believe, but she's more stunning after a full night's rest than she was when I'd watched her in my rearview mirror the entire time I'd driven us home. It's a small miracle I didn't wreck from my lack of attention on the road.

She struggles for a beat before finally sharing, "I remember being in the woods. There was someone there with me. Three others, I believe. One minute they were worried over keeping me safe, and the next... well, I don't remember anything afterward. My mind is fuzzy. It's frustrating."

My brow wrinkles at her words, attempting to make sense of them, yet I can't. Was she running from something? I found her alone, no others were around her. Were they really attempting to keep her safe? And why her?

"I woke up with your mouth on mine..." she trails off as the flush spreads over her throat.

She's so sweet and innocent, it has every protective instinct in me rearing to the surface. "You weren't breathing, and your heartbeat was nearly non-existent. I was, well, I was worried you'd die if I didn't help you."

"You were breathing air into me," she states, almost making it sound like a question. Her naiveté is endearing, and she speaks almost formally. Could she have belonged to the upper class and left for dead? Perhaps it was a ransom gone wrong? I'm going to drive myself mad with all the possibilities.

"Yeah, I was giving you CPR. Thankfully, it worked, and you began breathing again. It sounds odd being that we've only just met, but something about losing you sends a strong pang to my chest," I roughly admit and rub the spot above my heart. Pang is an understatement. When I thought she was dying, it felt like my heart was being ripped from my chest. Never have I experienced something so crippling in nature, especially since I don't know a thing about the woman.

I continue, "One of the guys recognized some of your symptoms. You were in the middle of a serious allergic reaction. Thankfully, he had an EpiPen and let me have it. I was shocked with how quickly it took effect." And grateful because I had no clue what was wrong with her. She's a beautiful enigma, one I want to figure out but probably shouldn't.

"Thank you for whatever you did to help me." She offers me a kind smile. The fairness of her milky flesh and regality of her features is like no other. The only name that suits her is Sleepy Beauty or princess, but I don't want to offend her by calling her pet names so soon. "What shall I call you?" she asks.

"It was my pleasure, and I'm Philip or Hunter, it's a nickname of sorts. You can call me either."

Putting my lips to hers was no difficult feat. I'd gladly do it again to see those enrapturing irises gaze at me full of gratitude. It'd be even hotter if I had her naked, pressed against a wall while I held her in place and tasted her mouth.

"My name is Aura. Will you tell me about finding me?"

I tip my head, drinking from my rich black coffee. "Nice to meet you." I lift my near empty glass and gesture. "Would you like some coffee?"

She shakes her head. "Only to learn the truth."

"All right then, come sit, and I'll tell you what I know."

CHAPTER 4

HUNTER

So I don't know much, but I let her in on what I can. Her gaze fills with confusion when I mention Viking's girl and how she was found. "You never saw anyone swimming or on the beach?"

She shakes her head. "No, I wasn't allowed to leave the wooded area. It wouldn't have been safe."

"Never?"

She shakes her head again, teeth sinking into her bottom lip. She's still a complete mess but gorgeous all the same. "I'm sorry, I can't remember much right now. The memories are there, but it's vague. I see images, but they don't make any sense. I'm hopeless, no help for you or your friends. Maybe you should just take me back. I don't want to displace you."

"You're not hopeless. You obviously went through a traumatic event, and your brain is either attempting to protect you or give you some more time to heal. I have a friend on the way to check you over. That island is the last place you need to be."

Fear strikes her orbs, and I rush to soothe it away. "It's just to make sure there isn't anything wrong. I helped you yesterday, but we need to know if there's more to it. I don't want anything to happen to you."

"But I don't know this person. What if they're the one who wants to harm me?"

She doesn't know me either. If she did, she probably wouldn't feel so at ease. "Are you afraid?" I'd think if she were scared of anyone, it'd be me, of all people. She knows little about the man sitting across from her, and it doesn't seem to bother her, only the thought of someone else encroaching in our cocoon of quiet false security.

"I have to be careful. It's the thing my mind keeps warning me about over and over."

"I'll keep you safe, that much I can promise you." *But maybe not from myself, that is.*

Her head dips in submission. She whispers, "I remember three women. I don't know who they are, but I think they may have helped me."

"Three women. That's a good start. Let the memories come back at their own pace, and please tell me about them whenever you're ready. Don't try to force anything, or it could take your mind longer."

"Okay, I'll try to let them come to me naturally."

I offer her an easy grin, hoping it brings her some comfort. "Now, how about a shower and some clean clothes?" I rake my gaze over her dirty, torn remnants of a dress. It doesn't cover much, and it's had my mind running wild with the possibilities of all those curves underneath the material. "Do you need any help?" I offer because she has memory loss, not because I'm planning on seducing her in the shower.

She nods. "Please."

"All right, follow me." I stand and offer her my palm. She places her hand in mine, allowing me to tug her down the hallway to the bathroom close to her bedroom.

This house has two, but the other is connected to my bedroom.

I show her where the soap and shampoo are and offer to grab the clothes I'd set out for her last night. She doesn't talk much, but I suppose with everything jumbled up in her mind, it's going to make her a bit quieter than usual women. I take my time grabbing the clothes, giving her a few minutes of privacy with the mirror. She seemed completely gobsmacked when she saw her image, and I wasn't trying to touch on that one. I have no clue what to say to put her at ease since she apparently wasn't anticipating the reflection she received.

The poor woman, I feel for her not knowing where she came from or who she is aside from a few surface-level details. At the same time, I worry about her for when the memories do return. Will they give her the hope and answers she needs, or will they be a nightmare putting her through whatever hell had attempted to kill her? She was in the middle of an allergic reaction, but everything around where I found her points to her running from someone. There's clearly more to her story than what I've discovered so far.

I head back to the bathroom. The door's ajar, so I don't hesitate to push my way inside. That's the first mistake I make. The second is when I can't seem to peel my gaze from her naked, lush curves. She stands before me, nude and unashamed about having every inch of her flesh on display for me.

"Oh shit," I murmur, distracted by her full breasts and curvy hips. The hair between her thighs is wild and free, and something about her being completely natural has me aching to put my hands on her. I wonder if a man's ever touched her before—pussy or otherwise.

"Thank you for the clothes," she eventually says.

I give myself a mental shake, pulling my gaze up to meet hers finally. "The door was open, I wasn't expecting—" I cut myself off and gesture to her body.

Her brows jump. "I left it open. Was that wrong?" she asks, so unbelievably innocent.

I swallow, my throat feeling dry. Who is this woman? And can I keep her? At least for a while? I could teach her so many things. I grit my teeth, the feeling of my hard cock clouding the rational thoughts from my mind.

With a gravelly edge to my voice, I reply, "Not wrong at all. I'll leave these here. Take your time." I set the clothes on the sink and tug a towel free from the rail. I push the material toward her, shielding her breasts. The moment she grabs it, I spin on my toes and hightail it to my bedroom. There's only one thing I can do that'll keep me from touching her like I want to—lube my right hand and use the mental image I can't seem to smother of her nakedness.

She's a fucking goddess.

She finds me on the back porch, drinking another cup of coffee. I needed the hot, bitter taste to keep my mind from constantly thinking of Aura. My clothes have swallowed up her feminine figure, and I nearly miss the tattered and torn rags she'd had tied on before. Maybe it's a good thing. I'm not sure I could handle her prancing around here in form-fitting dresses, the woman would drive me absolutely mad with lust.

"Do you know how long you were in those woods?" I start with, trying to put the important questions to the front of my mind. I need to figure out who this woman is and help her get back to wherever it is she should be.

She shakes her head, taking the seat next to me on the porch swing. "No," she admits, then says in a whisper, "It feels like it was a long time. I have a few memories of people who I think were my parents, but they don't make much sense."

"What about a last name?"

"A what?"

"Your name, is it short for anything? Do you have a first and last name?"

"My name's Aura. My father is Steven, and my mother is Lucia. I don't have any other names. This is frustrating." Her gaze clouds with tears, and I reach for her hand.

Giving it a tender squeeze, I relent. "It's okay. We don't have to push any of your memories. It'll happen when your mind is ready. Those names are a good start."

"Will you look for them?" Hope burns like embers in her irises, and the alpha inside me doesn't want to let her down, nor does it want me to let her out of my sight, but that's not realistic.

"Of course. Finding people is what I'm good at if you haven't guessed as much by now," I tease, making her smile through her few tears. My phone vibrates, drawing my attention away from the gorgeous woman at my side. I check the text, then stand and tug Aura with me. "My buddy, Briar, is here. He's the one I was telling you about. He'll check you out to make sure there's nothing else going on with you, medically speaking."

"Something inside is warning me to remain hidden. Should I be frightened?"

Pausing for a brief moment, I pull her to my chest and lightly wrap my arms around her frame. I murmur into her damp hair, "Remember what I said. I'll always protect you. Loyalty and promises aren't something I take lightly."

She inhales a deep breath, sighing against my chest as she nods her head in agreement. She fits against me perfectly, and the last thing I want to do is release her, but I must. Briar won't hurt her, he's one of the few I'd trust with my life. It's the same with all my brothers—they've proved their loyalty to me one way or the other, and the same goes for me with them.

I leave her to sit on the couch inside, staring out the large windows at the foliage behind the house. Something about it seems to calm her, which is exactly what she needs after whatever traumatic event she went through. I know there must be something, some sort of story behind what's happened. I can feel it. I tend to be right about these things.

"What's up, brother." I shake my buddy's hand and move back so he can step inside. "I appreciate you coming out here. I have a feeling you'll be able to gauge her well-being much more accurately than I can. I'm worried she's injured somehow and not telling me because she thinks it's normal or some shit."

"Don't sweat it, man. I don't mind the ride. It's so fucking peaceful out here."

"My castle in the hills."

"Lucky bastard. I need to find a place somewhere in the middle of nowhere to call my own."

I nod. "Aura's in here. She's nervous about being around other people. She doesn't speak much, and you'll have to pepper her with questions to get her to tell you anything."

"I'll go easy on her," he promises.

I knew I was making the right decision by calling him. "Aura, beauty, this is my buddy, Briar," I introduce them and assure her I'll be in the kitchen if she needs me. I don't want to distract them in any way since he may be able to get more information out of her than I can. He's had a lot of medical and mental health training, which is one of the main reasons why I wanted him to help me out with my bounty-hunting business. You never know when someone may get shot or stabbed, and he's the right guy to have on the job with you. He's also one hell of a listener when you need to talk about anything.

I top off my coffee, adding in a bit of Baileys, and sit at the counter, wired from all the caffeine I've consumed today. It makes my hands feel a bit jittery with the need to be busy. I pull my phone out and do a basic search on those three names together. I may as well be staring off into space, as the only thing I'm concentrating on is quieting my heart and breath enough to pick apart whatever scraps of conversation from Aura and Briar I can manage to catch. His voice is easy to pick up, but Aura's is the opposite—light and melodic.

I don't pay attention to how long I sit, but it feels like a while by the time Briar makes his way into the kitchen with me. My brows raise, wanting whatever diagnosis he's come up with. "Well?" I ask, picking away at a crack on the side of the countertop.

He heaves out a breath, moving to grab a bottled water off the counter. "Medically, she seems okay…"

"But? I can tell there's a but in there."

"Well, mentally, she's struggling. There's definitely some sort of trauma going on. I don't know what it is exactly and if it's the cause of her memory loss, but it'll likely take some time. She has a small knot on her head as well. She must've banged it against something at some point, but she can't recall when."

"She told me she thinks she was on that island for a really long time. I have a feeling her idea of time is way different than ours."

He nods. "I agree, based on the callouses on her hands and feet, she's definitely been living a life of work and weather. If she was hiding out in those woods like you believe, then there's no telling what she had to do to survive. Women like that appear weak, but it takes one helluva strong person to endure the elements, let alone whatever else she's lived through."

The theory makes my gut churn with unease. I despise the concept of her living through a life of struggle. She's far too sweet and young to have experienced that sort of life already. At least now, I can somewhat take care of her. She'll never have to go through whatever she did again as long as I'm by her side.

"I'm thinking she may have been kidnapped. At an early age, no less, her education seems almost nonexistent. She's smart, but in a self-taught sort of way."

I nod. "The thought had crossed my mind. I'm going to see what I can come up with on the kidnap end of things. It'd be a hell of a lot easier if I had a last name to go with, but I'll see if I can discover anything else about her."

"Keep me updated."

"I will, man, thanks again," I respond, already distracted by the search results pulled up on my phone with Aura's name in the headlines. I wish I could say I'm surprised, but the twisted truth of the matter is, I'm not.

CHAPTER 5

AURA

With each passing day, I grow a little more used to my surroundings and miss my previous life less and less. I don't know if it's wrong or right to feel this way, but I do. Hunter tells me not to worry about it. He says I should only concentrate on getting better and remembering what happened to me before he found me.

For some reason I trust him almost immediately—there's something about him that makes me feel safe. He's the one who saved me, after all, but from what exactly? I still have no idea. Not to mention he's beyond handsome and reminds me of the heroes in the books my father used to read to me. However, none of those heroes ever had any tattoos, scruff, or a voice that makes me clench with desire.

Eventually, I give in and begin to wear his clothes. They're too big but soft and warm, perfect for when I'm outside exploring. The outdoors brings me peace in such a confusing time, so I stay outside as much as possible. Hunter doesn't seem to mind either, as he'll often come out to the table to watch me as I smell and tend to his roses.

I still don't remember much of the events leading up to him and his brothers finding me, but I've managed to make some progress. For instance, now I can remember my three friends' names. They were more than just friends to me, more like family. I was separated from my parents at a very young age, and those three looked after me, taught me what they knew, and kept me safe for as long as they could. I know I should tell Hunter about them, but I've held back, hoping I'll remember details and more. I can't stand to see the look of disappointment on his face when I tell him I don't have all the answers. I know he wants to help me.

I'm grateful he stepped in and saved me but being so far away from my home is only making it harder for me to discover what I'm missing. I suppose I could panic over all of this, but that's not the way I was brought up. Before coming here, it was just the four of us, and all we had was each other to confide in and rely upon. I know there were times we had to hide away and be quiet, but now that I look back, I have no idea what exactly we were hiding from. It was just the way we did things. It was our life.

Does this mean that my mother and father are still alive? Not that I could ever find them, I haven't the faintest idea on where to even begin. Hunter is my best bet where finding and meeting people are concerned. He seems to be good at discovering information on just about anything. He's been nothing but kind and patient with me since I've been here, and I wish there were a way to show him how grateful I truly am for his help. I try to stay out of his way and not bother him often for anything. I feel guilty enough that I'm here using his things and eating his food without earning my keep. He doesn't seem to mind, but I'm used to working for everything. Nothing came easy on the island, and I don't expect it to be simple here either.

Living with him is another situation entirely. I've never shared a home with a man other than my father. Even then, I was far too young to recall much from our time aside from some sweet memories I cherish. Hunter is different—anytime I catch a glimpse of him with his shirt off, I have to take a moment to myself to get my bearings right once more.

I've had to fight myself every night from going to his room and crawling into his bed beside him. I'm not used to sleeping alone since we all snuggled together for warmth. The lack of skin-on-skin contact and the shared space have left me feeling lonely and a bit melancholy from time to time. I'm sure there's more to it since I find myself drawn to him more with each day. Now I'm struck with the new problem of wondering about my old life and what will happen in my future.

Before Hunter, my life was laid out quite simply. I knew I had to get up, do my chores, and worry about what the weather would bring. Now there's an endless array of possibilities and questions constantly filling my mind. 'What if' and 'why have' become the two main questions at the forefront of my mind. Rather than allowing myself to get upset over something I can't control, I do what brings me joy and lose myself amongst the roses.

HUNTER

Heading outside, I immediately search the area for Aura. She's been in my space for a while now, and I've grown used to her presence. I'm confident I've discovered who she is as well, but I've held back from telling her right away. I like her being here in my space, and I'm not ready to see her whisked away without a backward glance. It's selfish of me, but I'm keeping her safe. I won't hide the information I found from her forever. Just a little bit longer.

"I'm beginning to think you enjoy those rose bushes' company more than you do mine," I shamelessly flirt without coming on too strong. I want her to know I'm interested but not make her feel uncomfortable or pressured.

She offers a bright smile, one I've begun to look for more with each day. She's been coming out of her shell slowly but surely, and so far, I've adored every single layer of her personality she's shared with me.

Firing up the grill, I move to sit at the small iron table and wait for the burners to heat up. Aura joins me, sitting in the chair nearest me. I'm glad she's grown comfortable enough to be around me, and she no longer hesitates as she did in the beginning. I can feel her watching me and can't help but wonder what she thinks when she looks at me. Do I scare her like I have some in the past? I'm not exactly clean-cut—I'm more on the long-haired, scruffy-faced biker type. I rock my cut, leather jacket, jeans, and chains on the regular.

She hasn't asked me for a single thing since she's arrived and, in my opinion, it makes her all the more fascinating. I find myself aching to know every minuscule detail about her. My internet searches brought back details of her parents and their lives, but it's almost as if Aura was a ghost from a toddler on up. I should know since I watched her story unfold right from the beginning. She was reported missing, and all leads went cold on her whereabouts almost immediately. It's one aspect of her case that's always raised red flags for me.

Considering who her parents are, several red flags are popping up all over the place for me when I try to find out more details. Something about it all just doesn't add up. Not in the slightest, and I'm not ready for reality to come crashing down on our little bubble we've created. I can't believe, after all these years and being so close to the story, I didn't think of it sooner. Perhaps my nearness is what had me blinded to the possibility, but it could've been an inside job. I don't want to think that was the cause of her disappearance, but the more time I spend with her and re-reading the details of her case, the more it begins to make more sense.

"Why do you have shields tattooed on the tops of your hands?" she eventually asks. She's good with silence and just taking everything in, but she does have a curious side to her as well. I'm chalking it up to her being stuck on that godforsaken island for who knows how fucking long.

I hold my fists toward her and let out a chuckle, jokingly saying, "They're my virtue shields, I suppose." Yes, I've nicknamed my fists. Any man who deals in pain for a living has to, I guarantee it.

She offers me a sweet smile, not realizing that I use my fists as a means of protection and income. I defend myself when necessary, and due to my job, that's often. I can't help but wonder if she'd be terrified if she knew the type of man I am away from her. Would she run away, thinking I'm a monster of a man? She's naïve and tender-hearted and may not be able to handle the type of life I lead. I'm not ready to give her up just yet, not before I figure out what it is that draws me to her.

"And the others?" She gestures to the tattoos on my arms, and I flex, making her eyes grow wide. No doubt, she's been sheltered. I won't lie to myself and pretend that the way I affect her doesn't entice me further. She's everything any man would dream of having, myself included.

"Aura, my beautiful rose, your curiosity is my undoing," I admit with a grin and wrap her hand in mine. "Touch the one you want to know about." I bring her hand to my bicep, wanting, no, *needing* to feel her caress against my flesh. From the moment she parted her lids and gazed at me with those enrapturing irises, I knew I wanted her hands all over me. I'd never force her, but I can't help but dream of the day she reaches for me on her own, and I can bend her over to fuck her until she can't walk straight.

"This one." She lightly trails her fingertips over my inked timepiece and crown. Goosebumps pepper my skin as tingles begin in my cock. I'm going insane for this woman. It's become a chore not to walk around with a stiff dick twenty-four hours a day. "It's dark yet enchanting," she murmurs, drawing my gaze to her lips. They're perfect to take a cock. *Fuck. I have to stop imagining her like this.*

"Mmm, you should hear what my mother says about them. I was her crown prince at one time before I pulled up with ink on my flesh and a motorcycle between my thighs."

Her laughter tinkles over me, making my chest warm and feel tight at the sound. "Where did you learn to sing?" I change the subject to her, wanting to know anything I possibly can about the young woman I discovered unconscious in the woods. I heard her singing yesterday when she showered, then again, softly as she smelled every flower she could find in the yard. Contrary to what people say about shower singers, hers was a sound I couldn't get enough of.

"It was quiet where I grew up, and my friend often sang to me. It was something I picked up from her, I suppose."

"Your friend?"

"Yes, it came back to me this morning when I woke up. The three women I mentioned to you about being fuzzy, well, they were my friends. I lived with them."

"Any other memories surface?" I ask as guilt clouds its way into my gut. I should tell her about the family she has waiting for her nearby. I'm a selfish bastard for keeping what I know to myself. I promised I wouldn't allow anyone to hurt her, and right now, I have a sinking suspicion her family would be the first to blame.

She shakes her head. "Not yet, but I'm hopeful now. Did you see anyone else when you found me? There had to be others somewhere."

"No, but there were definitely more tracks. I picked up multiple sizes, so they belonged to different people."

"They must've been looking for me," she reasons as her features grow worried. "I hope they were, and nothing bad happened to them."

I cast her a tender gaze, wanting to set her mind at ease. "I don't think that was the case. A lot was happening on that island when my brothers and I were there. You looked like you'd been left alone for some time."

"But they loved me, I can feel it inside." She rests her hand over her heart, and the protector in me wants to make her forget about them completely.

"I believe you, and if you say one thing, then that's what we'll go on." I'm the last person who wants to break her heart and cause her pain. Everything I've been doing thus far has been to help and heal her.

"Do you think they left the island? Without me?"

Abandoned.

It's a viable prospect.

I shrug. "It's possible they escaped when everything was happening. It would've been chaos for them, I'm sure." I don't think they'd have gotten away without anyone noticing, but if they were able to stay on that island undetected for so long, anything's a possibility at this point. Clearly, everyone underestimated these women for them to survive off the land for so long as children.

I'll have to give the clubs a call sometime after Aura is asleep to find out if they've heard of anything more to do with that godforsaken island. "I'll see if I can find out more details. What can you remember about them? Were they older than you? Anything special about these people you have a feeling about?"

"They were older, but I don't know by how much. Laura was the oldest, and she always told me it was her job to keep me hidden and safe. She taught me what it means to be a woman and to be kind and helpful. Luna taught me all the songs she knew and helped me learn how to sing them. Mary made up the best stories. I fell asleep many times, listening to her talk with my head on her lap. I miss them."

I squeeze her hand, bringing it to my lips. I offer a kiss to her knuckles and promise, "I'll see if I can find them." At least I have more names to go on. I'll have to add them to Aura's and her parents to see if it brings up more leads. I have a feeling I know who they may be, but it's a long shot all of them would've survived together like she's saying.

It's hard to believe a wealthy, semi-famous botanical princess just disappears in thin air, and no one knows a thing. I've always suspected something was wrong with her case, no matter what everyone else claimed. I'm not buying it, and the detectives back then shouldn't have either. If they knew it was foul play and hid evidence, the brothers and I should pay them a little visit. Perhaps jog their memories with some persuasive techniques I like to use on people who cross me the wrong way and piss me the fuck off.

Could the three friends she's mentioned truly have been protecting her, or were they hiding out and made it seem like something else to Aura? There were despicable things happening on that island, and the three friends could've fled from there and taken Aura with them at any time. She'd have been tiny if she recalls being with them for so long. It'd have been difficult, but I suppose they could've pulled it off. How they were never discovered is another story entirely, one I'm far too adamant to learn about.

"The grill is on fire." She points out calmly.

"Oh shit." I jump to my feet and rush over. It's enough to distract me from my train of thought, and I let the subject go for now. I quickly get the grill under control and concentrate on making our dinner. I can't have my beauty starving—she already needs to put some meat on her bones.

My cell pings as a text comes through. It's late, another sleepless night filled with me tossing and turning. I can't seem to put my mind to rest with Aura in the house. My body craves hers something fierce, and it's taken everything in me not to act on my desires. Grabbing the device, I light up my screen and check the message. It's from Radge, and he needs my help with some mafia capos. It'll be bloody, but with everything else going on, it sounds like it's exactly what I need right now. I'll be able to take out my frustration on some fuckers giving him issues, so we'll both benefit from me heading his way.

I have Aura to worry about, though. Will she be able to stay alone? It appears she was on that damn island for years, but she wasn't completely alone. She's stronger than she first appeared, though, and besides, I shouldn't care so much. Why do I anyway? What's this weird hold she's had over me since the moment I had her in my arms? I'm too close to her case, too invested in the possible outcome.

It must be because I know who she is and haven't said anything to her. It has to be. I'm living with guilt weighing on my conscience, and I don't like it. Usually, I can effortlessly brush things off and move forward without a backward glance, but it doesn't feel right with her. There's also this drive inside me to dirty her up a bit, to show her what it's like to be with a man like me. Could she handle it? I'm not an easy guy, especially when it comes to fucking. I fuck hard and rough, and the last thing I want is to hurt her.

With a sigh, I move out of bed and cross to my closet. I begin tossing shit I'll need in a backpack. There's no way my thoughts will allow me to have any rest tonight. I shoot a text to my brothers, telling them to meet me at my house. I'll brief them on this next run, then by the time we're done discussing it and eat, we'll make it to Radge in plenty of time.

Let's hope Aura's okay with being left alone and waking to an empty house because she won't have much choice. I'm not letting her out of my possession just yet.

CHAPTER 6

AURA

Waking up to an empty house, there's an extra stillness to the air that's not normally here when Hunter's home. There's always some sort of small sound in the background, like the coffee maker or his music in the garage while he's detailing his motorcycle. I'll admit it's a bit overwhelming as I'm not used to being completely alone. I still take time to search through the house one room at a time, knowing they'll be empty before I ever enter the room. The sun's high, letting me know I slept much later than usual, and it's probably afternoon. I can't say I'm surprised. I've been restless sleeping alone. It's already strange enough getting used to the bed and the quiet as I'm used to the sounds of bugs and birds and other creatures of the night.

His bedroom is where I spend most of my time looking around. I can't help myself as it gives me a small glimpse into the man himself. There's not much in here. His clothes are neatly folded in his drawers with the thicker items hanging in his closet. I pick random garments and inhale deeply, hoping to catch a hint of his scent. It's useless as they all smell like the overly perfumed detergent he keeps in the laundry room. I don't want to smell fake scents, I want his.

Moving along in my perusal, I take note of the books on his nightstand. I have no idea what the titles say, but I'm sure they're full of action. Would it be weird if I laid in his bed? Rather than dwell on the heavy question, I let myself lay down in his spot. I know it belongs to him because the indention in the pillow gives him away.

Turning on my side, I press my face into the soft black material and breathe deeply. I'm hit with the scent I've grown to associate as Hunter's. The smell is outdoorsy yet clean. It's entirely his own, and I find myself not wanting to move. This is exactly what I was searching for. I know I can't stay here forever, so I stand, and with a final glance toward his spot, I head for the door.

Eventually, I discover a note with small scratchy writing that I assume belongs to Hunter. I'm grateful he attempted to let me know where he was going, if only I knew how to read. He could leave notes all over the place, but none of it would do me any good. Rather than allow myself to freak out, I decide to head to the one place that gives me peace—the outdoors. The house is completely locked up, and much to my surprise, a shrill alarm alerts the moment I open the door leading out to the back patio.

The piercing sound scares me badly enough I want to fall to my knees, curl up in a small ball, and wait for it to stop. I begin to do just that, but the noise never wavers. With the door wide open, I do the one thing I can to stop the chaotic noise. I run. My feet pound against the dense forest floor, and with each step, the haze clouding my vision eases.

After a while, I stop. I'm far enough away to hear the annoying alert, but not for it to frazzle me like before. Unsure of what to do next, I lean back against a huge tree, tuck my legs into the oversized shirt, and wait. Hunter will come for me eventually.

HUNTER

"Fuck!" I hiss as the text alert comes through, letting me know my house alarm has been activated. There's no way for me to contact Aura. I haven't gotten another cell for her nor showed her how to use one.

My cell rings as the alarm company calls. "Yeah?"

"Sir, we've had an alert coming from your home. Do I need to send assistance?"

"Tell me which sensor?" I have a very elaborate system, and this guy should be able to tell me details.

"Your passcode, sir?"

"0990."

"Thank you for confirming. The alert seems to be the back door. Shall I send the police?"

"No. I'll handle it."

"Do you want me to shut the alert off inside the home?"

"No. If someone has entered unwelcome, I want them to feel the pressure of the noise and lights."

"All right. Please let us know if we can be of assistance."

I hastily hang up, shoving my cell in my cut's pocket, and take off in the direction of my house. I wasn't too far away, having stopped to fill up with gas before saying goodbye to my brothers after our last job for Radge. It was a quick, bloody trip, but satisfying, nonetheless. My thoughts drown out the roar from my pipes as I press the bike's engine harder to get back to Aura. If anyone came for her while I was gone, I'll bleed them out.

I'm hoping it's my little beauty who unknowingly set off the alarm, rather than someone there after her or me. I'm to blame if I've left her there in the path of danger. My gut churns with a new dose of guilt, and I swallow, choking the sensation down, putting it away for another time. I should've prepared her better for my time away or had someone from the club stick close by if she needed help. A prospect could've kept an eye on her.

The thought of anyone else protecting or touching her for any reason sends ice spiraling through my veins. I'd fucking murder them, brother or not. There's something deeply rooted in my chest when it comes to that woman. It's the craziest shit I've ever experienced, this insatiable need to protect and own another human being, and I have merely just begun when it comes to her.

I've heard bullshit before about love at first sight and soulmates, and it's all the talk of foolishness. This isn't love or something as trivial as such. This is lust and primal need taking over every rational part of my being, not to mention we have a history that's been twisted together since we were children. She was always meant to be mine, but she doesn't know that yet. She will, though.

Pulling into my driveway, I notice the lack of disturbance. The alarm's still blaring its piercing siren, and the lights around the outside perimeter are all flashing. Leaving my motorcycle behind, I quickly head in the front door on a mission. Storming through the house, I check every room over for Aura, but she's nowhere in sight. This could be good or bad—either she's the reason for the alarm or someone has taken her.

I deactivate the alarm and carefully step out the back, being as quiet as possible. I yank my gun from the holster as I flick my gaze over the backyard. Most of my property is surrounded by trees and nature, creating a natural camouflage for anyone with an untrained eye.

With light steps, I track the footprints leading into the foliage. Thankfully, there's only one set and knowing as much, has my heart rate beginning to calm the fuck down. Aura is a smart girl, that much is certain. Was she running from someone? Or was she running to get free of me? Either way, I'll find her or them, whichever, and dole out punishment as needed.

She's intelligent in survival, and she's not dangerous or stupid. I place my weapon back in the holster since I won't need it when it comes to her. If she were running from somebody else, they haven't come this way, that much I'm certain of. They'd have to be a fucking ninja not to leave a twig unturned in their haste, and either way, I can pull my knife in a heartbeat. The path I'm following was created by someone small and in a rush. It was Aura, I'd know her presence anywhere at this point. I'm not sure what makes her so different from others, but there's something special there.

I catch a glimpse of her form hiding behind a large tree. She's tucked into herself, making her appear tiny with hands over her ears, silently rocking.

This explains everything. She must've triggered the alarm, and the noise freaked her out. No longer hiding my steps, a large stick cracks under my boot, the sound practically echoing amongst the quiet shield of nature. Aura's spine straightens ramrod straight, and in the next breath, she's sprinting from her spot. She's fast, I'll give her that.

My poor woman is spooked—scared of the world and its sounds she's been kept away from. Seeing her run has my primal instinct to pursue and conquer, consuming my rational thoughts, and I give chase. She may be tiny and quick, but I've been tracking people my entire life. Whether it be for a beatdown when I was younger or now hunting down a runner to collect the hefty bounty on his head.

I get close enough to nearly touch her back as she runs, and I leap for her. My arm hooks around her waist, locking her to me, and I fall backward, her on top of me, so she's not hurt in the process. Her limbs flail, her adorable fierce tiger kitten side coming out to fight me off. I have her flipped over and on her back, pinned underneath me before she can get her first bit of my flesh in her grip. *Fuck, she's beautiful.*

I'm breathing hard, panting, as my nose lines up with hers. Adrenaline spirals through my blood, making my heart beat wildly, pumping with excitement. Her eyes widen as they take me in, her chest bouncing with her heavy breaths.

"H-Hunter?" she eventually stammers, relief filling her gaze.

"Mmm," I answer with a growl deep in my chest. I'm fucking hard as a rock, my cock throbbing for her in my jeans. I can't remember craving someone this intensely, ever. She smells absolutely delectable, her pheromones calling me in to take what I desire.

Unable to hold myself back, my mouth claims hers.

Finally.

It's forceful, hard, and quick. My tongue demands entrance, and she relents, parting her lips for me. With the first feel of her tongue against mine, a moan escapes my eager kiss. My knees relax, no longer wanting to hold my weight from hers. I fit between her legs so comfortably, my cock heavy with desire as I rest it against her heat. She was made for me, every curve and valley fitting me like a glove.

She releases the sweetest little groan, and with it, I thrust my hips, rubbing my hardness against her soft sex. Fuck, I want her. I crave her pussy like nothing else—she's temptation in the sweetest form of torture. I pull my mouth away, leaving enough room to rasp against her perfect lips. "You run from me, you become prey. Do you understand that, little girl?" I warn, making her eyes flutter open once more and widen with my promise.

She dips her head in a quick nod, licking her lips as she looks me over. I haven't brought myself to move off her just yet—she feels far too good. I push my hips against her pussy again, enjoying as she draws in a quick gasp, and her irises light with desire. "Hunter," she whispers my name, and fuck, she may as well be a siren.

I brush our lips against one another. Not in a kiss, but a caress filled with promises I'm not yet ready to voice. One kiss is all I can handle right now, anything more, and I'll be fucking her here and now in this very spot. She's not ready for raw and dirty, or we'd already be naked like animals in heat.

"Time to go back home." I pull myself up with a deep exhale and reach for her. She places her palm in mine and allows me to help her up. I don't drop it as I lead her toward my house. "Want to explain what the fuck you were doing out here, hiding, while the alarm was going off? You left the back door wide open, and anyone could've gotten to you."

"I woke up and wanted to go outside to the flowers, but when I opened the door, that scream sounded, and it scared me. I ran and hid, not sure what was happening."

I nod, not looking at her. I need to put some distance between us to think straight again. "The house alarm is so no one breaks into the house while I'm gone. I told you to stay inside last night before you went to bed. You should've listened to me."

I make out her frown in my peripheral vision but ignore it. I raced back here, thinking she could possibly be hurt, brutalized, or killed only to find out it was merely because she wanted to smell the flowers. "You may have been shrouded in a false sense of safety while hiding out on that island, but this is the real world, and it's filled with ugly monsters. There were terrible men on that island with you as well, but I'm guessing you were one of the lucky ones and never found that out."

"Why are you being this way? Have I upset you?"

I round on her, shoving her against a tree as I loom over her. My stare takes her in from head to toe, wanting to scold her, but I catch the blood on her feet, the scratches on the sides, and I can imagine what the bottoms must look like. With an angry growl, I scoop her into my arms, making her cry out in surprise.

"You're bleeding," is all I say as I stomp the rest of the way to the house. I think I scare her as she quietly watches me, without attempting to escape my hold. It's a good thing. I don't know if I could handle the thought of her injuring herself more, all because I decided to give chase, hunting her down like she's my next mark, and then fucking her in the middle of the woods.

"Why am I here if you won't speak to me?" she questions, ignoring my frown as we get inside, and I spin around. I reach for her throat, yanking her face to mine. I can't seem to stop touching her. I shouldn't be so aggressive. Who knows what all she's been through, but she stirs up my every emotion. It has me feeling like I'm losing control, and any lack of control doesn't bode well with me at all.

"You're right, you don't understand anything." I want to beat on my chest and demand she stay here for as long as I desire. It'll only backfire if I do, though.

Rather than say anything, my mouth slams on hers. I kiss her like I'm starved for her, a man dying for a sweet taste of her lips. And fuck me if she isn't the sweetest sip of water I've ever tasted. There's no going back after this. I know it, and she will soon enough.

CHAPTER 7

AURA

He kissed me. I'm not sure how I feel about it. Of course, I've wanted it to happen, but dreaming of something versus it actually happening are two completely different things. I'm confused. I was around the same three people for most of my life, and now my world's been turned upside down. I still haven't heard from my friends, nor has Hunter mentioned anything regarding them. For all I know, they could've left without me, or even worse, they could be dead. The possible notion of them being out of this world forever sends pain straight to my heart.

I can't think of them right now as I have other things on my plate at the moment. The kiss from Hunter doesn't help, as they're the only other people I've ever kissed before. For example, there's this undeniable chemistry between Hunter and me as well as discovering who my parents are.

I'm torn on finding out what happened to me if I was lost or taken. Then again, I can't help but wonder if the truth will break me. At this rate, anything is possible, and I'm just grateful Hunter was there on the island when I needed him. Regardless, I can't depend on him to always be there. I need to rely on myself as I could on the island. I was taught to be self-sufficient, to work hard, and earn my keep the same as everybody else. In a perfect place, that would be enough, but this feels like a new world completely, and I have to relearn everything. I feel useless, and I hate it.

He scared me when he found me hiding against the massive tree, even though I knew he was coming and to expect him. It's what he does—he hunts people, and he's good at it. I wasn't anticipating his fury, the weariness in his eyes when my gaze met his. I was responsible for putting the look on his face, and it crushed me inside. The last thing I'd ever want to do is upset him in any way, but it couldn't be helped. I had to get away from the shrill noise. If he hadn't activated it, then I would've stayed close to the house.

No matter how many times I go over the events in the past twenty-four hours, I keep coming back to the moment where his mouth was on mine. I've never felt something so bone-deep as if his lips were made solely for mine. I'm a fool for dreaming up such things and that he could be the one person meant for me. Who knows if that concept even exists and if true love is 'the real thing.' I've been kept away from society and its norms for far too long to know what fact or fiction is when it comes to love. I want to believe it'll happen like in the many stories I've been told over the years, but if my feelings for Hunter are any indication, then it's best to expect the unexpected.

I've apologized time and again since everything happened, but he's been more concerned with the cuts on my feet. Not only is he a hunter, but he's a protector and provider. I'm fine, just a few shallow scrapes and bruises, but they always heal quickly, unlike the scars of the heart.

With those thoughts, I pick through the vague memories of my parents again, attempting to squeeze out every detail possible. I want to remember what my father was like, his temperament and mannerisms. Would he respect Hunter or be against the semblance of friendship we've forged? I'd like to believe he'd approve of him, but there's no true way of knowing. The only thing I'm certain of is he'd want me to survive this overwhelming, scary new place I've merely begun to discover.

Needing to be close to Hunter again, I make my way through the house, ready to find him and put this behind us once and for all. We're both adults, and there's no reason to keep any lingering tension between us. We seem to be walking a fine line between anger and passion—either we're going to fight or fuck—his words, not mine.

I'll never forgive myself if I've ruined our friendship all because I was overcome with a moment of irrational fear. I have to finish remembering everything and no longer be a burden to the man I consider my savior.

HUNTER

As much as I'd prefer to have my way with Aura, I refrain. It's not an easy feat when she draws me to her like a moth to a flame. She's the flower, and I'm the bee, ready to pollinate her sexy ass and then some. I've already made the mistake of kissing her, and it nearly tipped me over the edge of no return. It's far too fucking easy to lose myself in her, and I can't allow myself to be swept away. Something doesn't sit right with me on everything, but my gut tells me I won't know exactly what it is until I allow her to return home—not to the island and not here, but to her parents. I don't want to let her go, but I'm going to have to, eventually.

Lying in bed, it's another long, sleepless night full of tossing and turning. Knowing Aura is right down the hall is an alluring tease that seems to have a penchant for keeping me up at night. I've lost more sleep from thinking of this woman than I have over anyone else, combined. Ever since the day in the bathroom when I walked in on her naked, I can't seem to wash the image from my mind, nor do I want to. I know what she has underneath those oversized, borrowed clothes of mine, and it's done nothing but torment me ever since with all the possibilities of what I could do with her.

"Hunter?" My fantasies of the woman standing in my doorway come to a screeching halt. It's bad enough I've broken a sweat, but if she comes close enough, she'll get an eyeful of my stiff dick. This isn't how I anticipated any of this would go with her, not at all.

"Mmm," I reply with a frustrated grunt. I shift my leg up, the angle helping to hide away my throbbing length.

"Are you awake?" her sweet melodic voice asks, still too shy to just waltz into my room.

"Not by choice," I murmur, cracking my lids open enough to gaze at her, yet not be blinded by the hall light she's flicked on.

"I can't sleep either. Not since…"

"Since what?"

"Earlier. You know when we…"

Ah. She's either too nervous or reluctant to say it outright. "Tell me, Aura, have you ever kissed another man before?" I'm a glutton for punishment and need to know.

She shakes her head.

"Answer me," I demand gruffly.

Her mouth gapes open briefly, then she shifts, standing to her full height. She's got a backbone in her. I assume she's just not used to showing it. "No."

"No other men or no other person? Ever?"

"I've kissed my friends, sure, but it wasn't quite as intense. Our kiss was different."

Intense. Yep. Good word for what was exchanged between us in the woods. Discovering she's never kissed another man has my desire for her skyrocketing to another level entirely. "What are you doing up?" I can't help but sound grouchy. She's in my doorway wearing nothing but my long shirt. I can see her stiff nipples, for Christ's sake, and I want to taste each one. It'd drive any man with a lick of sense nutty inside. Lord knows my cock's already on lockdown wanting to claim the bitch.

"I thought I heard you."

"Liar. Try again."

She sighs, glances around, and stares at me on my bed for a beat. I'm about to turn over and give her my back when she takes a step in my direction. I pause, eyes locked on her as she strides toward me, peeling off the shirt. She lets it fall to her feet, forgotten, as she makes her way to me. I quietly groan at her silhouette. It's been too long since I've fucked a woman, and she's only making it harder to resist the temptation she imposes.

"I don't like sleeping alone," she finally admits, climbing into my bed, stark naked. I was right, she doesn't wear panties or boxers under those shirts she's borrowed. A man's nemesis is a sexy woman wearing his shirt with nothing on underneath. It'll bring the strongest guy straight to his knees for you.

Nearly choking, I'm taken off guard but manage to swallow it down without making myself look like a total jackass. I've had plenty of women before, so no reason to get all jittery around this one. Only, she's special, at least she is to me. I look at her knowing she was meant to be mine from the start, yet I can't do anything about it, and the knowledge teases me each time it passes through my mind. I'm left in this strange sense of limbo, attempting to be the better guy and do the right thing when everything in me strains to do what I desire.

Lying stock still, I watch her as she makes herself comfortable in my bed. Kicking her off is absolutely out of the question. I was literally just wishing she was in my bed, and now here she is. I'd be an idiot to tell her to go back to her room. It's crazy I've come to think of the guest room as her private space. I've never lived with a woman before her, but surely, they all need their own room. Kind of like guys having the garage or those elaborate closets I've seen women have on design shows. They're massive with chandeliers and shit, and the same Aura would have if she were home, no doubt.

She lays on her side facing me, staring at my lips enticingly, making me want to lean over and kiss her once again. This time around, I wouldn't stop so suddenly but prolong it and savor the feel of her mouth pressed to mine. I watch as she licks her lips, saliva pooling on my tongue at the thought of tasting her—not only her tongue but her pussy. Aura's everything good and sweet in the world, so there's no doubt in my mind that her pussy tastes like a sinful dose of heaven.

A contradiction does suit her, though. She's innocent and almost timid yet wants to be fucked like a bad girl. I can read it all over her features, and fuck, if it isn't the true test of my will. Every minute with her, the struggle to keep my hands to myself becomes harder. Just like my fucking cock at the moment. Her in my bed, naked and wanting, will drive even the saintliest of men mad with untamed lust.

"What do you want, Aura?"

It's taking everything in me to keep her stare when I want to be ogling every glorious inch of her full tits. She flutters her lashes, sending me a coy look. I know what she wants, she doesn't need to say it, but I'm still going to make her. This is wrong, her here in my bed when I know so much and haven't told her anything. I push the thoughts to the back of my mind as she whispers, "I want you."

"Me, huh? Do you have any idea what you're asking me for?"

"Yes. I want you to touch me all over my body. Make me feel good. Please?"

She doesn't need to tell me twice as exploring her pale silky flesh will be an easy feat. Reaching toward her, my fingertips fall to her shoulders first. I want to feel her everywhere—every single inch of her. Where to begin is the hard part, but her bare shoulders are an extremely alluring piece of her. I caress her skin there, lightly drawing my fingers down over her arm and then back up. Goosebumps pepper her milky tone, and I relish knowing I've gotten a response from her so easily. She's responsive and will make this all the more enjoyable for both of us.

"Can I touch you as well?"

She wants to touch me? Her words send a sharp spike of desire straight to my throbbing cock. I'm so hard, my length begs to be set free, and she wants to know if she can touch me?

"Fuck," I curse with a sigh.

What do I say to her? I want to rough her up a bit, squeeze her, pluck at her nipples, and maybe command her to jump on my cock and ride me like she's never ridden before. However, I don't want to scare her off so quickly, not when I have her this close. There's no doubt in my mind she wouldn't know how to deal with me if I went full-on right off the bat. So rather, I say, "You can touch, and you don't need to ask me. You always have my consent."

She releases a tense breath. It comes out as a sweet, excited sigh. Her warm exhale has fantasies consuming my mind of feeling it, along with her lips exploring my body and my dick.

My free hand moves to her throat, my grip wrapping around and holding firm while my other fingertips move to her breast. My thumb rotates in circles over her pert, dusky peach nipple. My palm cups the heavy flesh as I alternate from squeezing and teasing the peak. My eyes lock with hers, not breaking the stare as I lean in and place my mouth around the perky nub. My tongue eagerly swirls as my teeth lightly bite down with enough pressure to cause her to squirm with longing.

Her cheeks flush, her chest moving quicker as she begins to pant. She wants me as much as I do her. I lean back, letting the flesh pop free from my mouth and move to show her other breast the same amount of attention. She pulls a groan from me as her hand seeks out my length, and she gives me a quick tug. When she asked to touch me, I was banking she'd go for my chest or my hair, where chicks always head to first. Not her, though, she's less inhibited and going right for the good part.

If she wants surprises, I'll give her one. My hands move to her hips, and in the next second, I have her up and over me and spun around, so her pussy is right in front of my face. Eagerly, I lick my lips and gaze at the wet, swollen pink flesh. She's already drenched, and I've barely begun to touch her. My index finger moves to trail through her soaked slit, coating the tip in her sweet-smelling juices.

Not being able to hold back, I suck the wetness between my lips. Her flavor explodes on my tongue while her scent surrounds me, and I eagerly watch her cunt leak more fluid. I've never wanted to be inside a pussy so much in my goddamn life.

Using the tips of two fingers, I rim her entrance, dipping just enough inside she feels me there. She's enticing in all the right ways. "Is this okay?" I ask, wanting her to be secure enough she can tell me no at any time if she needs to.

"Yes, please do it more."

"How much have you done before?" I can't help but ask—everything with her has me curious and edging for more information.

"My friends and I, we used to touch each other at night before bed. When we swam or bathed, then we'd lick each other sometimes as well."

"Fuck," I release on a breath. I'm about to be sent over the edge just from picturing what she's telling me. "They... uh... touched you too?"

"Yes, and we had a soft stick that was bigger than our fingers we could use if we wanted to."

Precum leaks from my tip as I imagine her taking a small, smooth piece of driftwood and using it to pleasure herself. They were on that island alone for far too long, but even in their circumstances, they found ways to enjoy themselves and each other. She probably knows more about her sexuality than any other woman I've ever had the opportunity of fucking.

"Jesus," I pant. "No man has ever been inside this pussy? Only fingers, tongues, and toys?" I ask, needing her to continue building up my visual. It appears my fantasy can't compare to the real thing, and she has me on edge.

"No man has ever touched me like this, only you," she admits and sends me on another level of possessiveness. She was meant to be mine from the start of our lives, and this is only more proof that the world agrees.

"You're so sexy, Christ. You really have no idea, do you?" I lean in, deeply breathing in her scent and lick her from ass to clit. She moans and tugs on my cock again. "Don't stop," I order, repeating her words from earlier.

"Can I lick you too? Would you enjoy it?" she asks so innocently, I nearly come unglued right then and there.

"Y-yes," I choke out. "Lick all you want." She doesn't hesitate, her mouth surrounding my length as she begins to lightly suck on my tip. "Oh." I clench my teeth together, silently begging for stamina and patience to make sure she enjoys herself fully before I come all over the damn place like a novice.

All the filthy thoughts running through my mind ache to fall from my lips, but I somehow manage to bite most back. I've never been anyone's first at anything before, the notion urging me on to beat on my chest a bit in triumph. It probably means nothing to her, but it certainly caves a chink in the invisible armor surrounding my heart where she's concerned.

"Damn, your mouth feels like heaven," I offer, encouraging her so she doesn't stop.

She takes my compliment in stride, eagerly keeping pace with my tongue. My fingers thrust deep, my thumb steadily applying pressure on her clit until she explodes.

CHAPTER 8

AURA

My body shatters for him while my noisy moans fill the room. The sensation of floating hits me everywhere as do the fiery zings of my pussy clamping onto his digits, begging for more. My body milks the orgasm for as long as possible, my head spinning with relief. Sleepiness would usually overtake me in other circumstances, but with Hunter, I simply desire more. I want all of him, filling me everywhere. Too much, too soon? I hope not because I'm all in for this.

My hands move, twisting and turning as I continue to work him over. "Does this feel good?"

"Fuck, yes. You have no idea what your touch does to me."

"I want you inside me, please." I give his length an extra tight squeeze and grin when he responds with a groan. Taking his length deeper in my mouth, I suck with more force. His hands clench my thighs as he pants through each pass my mouth makes over his cock.

After a few beats, he leans back, smirking as his cock pops free from my mouth. "You're sure about this? I don't want you to feel like you need to do this for me to allow you to sleep in my bed."

"Ever since you kissed me in the woods, I've thought of nothing else… only you touching, kissing, and filling me repeatedly."

"Jesus," he swears to himself and leaps from the bed. He rifles through the top drawer of his bureau where I'd found his box of condoms in my exploration. I'd heard of them before in a few of the spicier stories Mary would tell us at times. She had a hard life before she was adopted and learned things far too young. Hunter staggers back to the bed, hands busily tearing through the package and rolling the latex over his shaft.

Wanting to touch him as quickly as possible, I eagerly reach for him. One hand lands on his shoulder while the other falls to his broad chest. He's built like a dream—all hard angles but still soft enough to cuddle up to. My palms glide over his heated flesh, taking in the smattering of light brown hair over his chest. It's thin but still enough to know he's a man's man and doesn't believe in a smooth finish. I've heard men's bodies are all different, just like women's, and to witness one for the first time in my life has my gaze widening with excitement.

"You're beautiful," I comment, drawing a startled glance from him.

"You're the stunning one," he argues. His fingers glide through my long locks, tilting my head backward as he leans in. His lips pepper my tender skin with kisses and an occasional lick. I like to imagine he's tasting me, saving my flavor to memory as I've been doing with him. This is something I never want to forget, no matter if it happens in the future—this time will always be extra special for me.

"Touch me." I'm ready to beg, my body's vibrating to feel him inside and against me.

"Don't have to tell me twice," he responds on a growl. His head dips lower, taking my breasts in his mouth. Somehow, it feels better this way—perhaps it's in the way he sucks them so forcefully. My thighs clench as wetness floods me below. I grip onto his shoulders, afraid I may collapse into a wanton heap if he keeps it up.

"Yes, that feels remarkable," I mutter. He goes to his knees, his lips trailing over my abdomen. His mouth parts as his teeth make their presence known. Small bites have me bowing my head to watch him as he moves inch by inch lower. He kisses down my thigh, then back up the opposite, only to punctuate it by sucking my clit. A scream rips free at the intense sensation. Him going from soft to straight on has my body lost in how to respond.

"Please, more," I begin to unnecessarily plead. He's giving me what I desire, but I'm too impatient to wait. I want it all, right this moment.

Ignoring my begging, he circles behind me and gently kisses up the back of my legs. He nips at the skin behind my knee, and I nearly buckle over. I'm learning the spot is sensuous and underestimated. Hunter's a skilled lover, and I won't be doubting as much after his exploration. More kisses glide up the backs of my thick thighs with bites on each of my butt cheeks. I can't help but moan and giggle at the same time. He smacks my behind enough not to hurt but warn me to stop the giggling. "Oh!" I breathe hard as the slap turns me on just as much as the sucking did.

"You were made to be cherished. Designed for a man who wouldn't undervalue every single inch of you," his deep voice whispers at the back of my neck. Shivers and goosebumps skate over my flesh, making my nipples stand even firmer than before.

"Touch me, Hunter."

He growls at my mention of his name, then his strong arms are surrounding me from behind. "Shall I fuck you like this? Bend you over and slide my long, thick cock into you from behind? Think you could handle me all at once?" He breathes against my ear, and my eyes roll heavenward.

"I'll handle you some way, I promise as much."

"Christ," he hums, then spins me to face him. His mouth is on mine before I can blink. His lips press to mine, tongue parting them to explore. One hand holds me securely to his frame while the other brokers our fall onto the oversized bed. He pulls back just enough to whisper, "I won't hurt you the first time I take you. We'll save that for another if you want it."

"Oh, I want it," I whisper without thinking. He could fill me from behind right now, but I won't fight him on it if he wants to wait. At this point, I couldn't care less as long as he's in me some way. The thought of him filling me as I desperately crave has me eager for anything he'll offer.

Our mouths move together as our bodies writhe against each other, searching for some semblance of pleasure with a bit of pressure. Our hands tangle as we both eagerly move to touch and tug as quickly as possible. Whoever can wait and take their time must be a saint because there's no way I can prolong the sweetest sense of torture for long.

"Fill me," I quietly demand, and he groans, his forehead resting against mine.

His eyes clench closed as he breathes deeply. Eventually, he admits, "You have me worked up and ready to explode. This may be much shorter than I want it to be."

I pull his cock toward my entrance and reassure him, "I don't care how long it lasts, only that it happens." It's what he needs to hear as his hand eagerly moves up his length, positioning him right where I need to feel him most. His free hand moves to the bedspread beside me as he braces himself, then slowly begins to work his cock into my entrance.

He stretches me to the point I feel full. There's no pain, only relief. I can't help but think he was made for me, and he belongs there and nowhere else. I'm his home, and he's mine. All this time away, and it was him I've been missing.

"Are you all right?"

I nod, only to realize he's waiting for my words. I meet his concerned gaze and offer a tender smile. "I'm more than okay, I'm great."

He smirks and begins to move. It feels amazing, not only his length filling me but the warmth coming off his frame. His presence surrounds me, and it's enough to have me biting my lip and closing my eyes. He's everywhere all at once, and it's better than I've ever dreamed of.

"Hold on to me. Look at me and let me know you feel me," he orders.

My eyes shoot open, colliding with his blazing irises. One hand moves to grip his butt while the other hooks under his arm to grip his shoulder blade. He's strong, sculpted with muscles I didn't know a man possessed.

"Much better. You want it slow and soft or hard and fast? Your pussy grips me so perfectly, it has me seeing stars already."

I love his abrupt honesty. "Fast," I choke out as he plunges forward, rocking my world. He's not the only one seeing stars as he pistons in and out, swiveling his hips left then right. "Yes! Oh, my," I moan far too loudly to be acceptable, but he doesn't seem to mind.

"You're so wet." His fingers find my clit, and I'm done for. Another orgasm explodes through me, shaking me all over. "Fuck, yes," he groans, following me into bliss.

HUNTER

"It's time for you to see your family," I eventually make myself admit aloud, even though it pains me to say it. The last thing I want to do is let her go, and then, God forbid, something happens to her. I've grown used to her being here, comfortable with our arrangement. The sex helps. I am not going to lie, but I'm a man, and enjoying her body has been put to the forefront of my mind. Of course, there are feelings involved behind the carnal pleasure, but we're not at the stage yet where we admit them. At least, I'm not. Fucking is one thing but acknowledging it aloud how I'm falling for her is another thing entirely.

"You've found them?" she asks, her eyes growing wide with wonder and excitement. Should it wound my pride to see her so happy over leaving me for them? My ego's going to take a hit with her taking off, but I have to remind myself this isn't about me and my needs. It's about Aura, and it has been from the beginning. She's ready, and it's past time I bring her to her family.

Oh yeah, so I haven't exactly told her about her family and all I know about them. I couldn't bring myself to utter a word about any of them before now. I'm selfish, wanting to keep her all to myself like I have, but I'd do the same thing again if I had another opportunity to. They may be her family, but they're not good enough for her sort of soul-deep beauty.

It's hypocritical of me to think so, considering I'm basically on the opposite end of the spectrum as far as good men are concerned. I've killed people. Not only one or two, but many. My hands are dirty, stained in blood as is my soul. The kicker is I'm too far gone for her to care about any of it. I'll lie and cheat, kill and maim, whoever I have to, to make sure she remains safe. Aura leaving my property has me worried. I can control the outcome of a threat here, but in the outside world, it's not quite as easy. Her family's loaded, too, a botanical empire she sits at the top of and has no clue of. It'll only add to the allure of harming her, of using her for whatever some asshole can get his hands on.

"Your parents have missed you, I'm certain of it. I haven't contacted them yet on your behalf, I wanted to discuss it with you first. Once you give me the okay, I'll reach out." Silently, I beg her to tell me what I want to hear, how she wants to stay here away from everyone else, alone with only me. It's a stretch, but still, my heart reaches for hers, claiming it as my own.

"This is amazing news, Hunter. Thank you for finding them! I-I can't wait to meet my parents." She throws herself at me, wrapping me in a warm embrace. Her nose burrows into the spot between my shoulder and throat, making me shiver. It's a sensitive place, not that it matters at the moment. My mind's too busy flip-flopping all over the place, scatterbrained with all the things I know can possibly hurt her. Her general well-being has been pushed to the forefront of my priorities, along with her happiness, and this screams danger zone.

"They'll be lucky to have you," I murmur instead, fighting the twisting sensation in my stomach. I hold onto her tightly, not wanting her to lean back and be able to read all the raw emotion reflecting in my irises over her excitement.

"They'll want me?" Her tone grows unsure, and I want to do anything I can to expunge whatever thoughts plague her at the moment.

"Of course, they will. They didn't stop looking for you. Your parents never gave up on the possibility of you returning to them someday."

"I'm so happy. Thank you for all you've done for me. I'll never forget you."

Then why does it feel like she already has with her statement? "You can always count on me, I give you my word."

"And your word is everything," she repeats what I'd previously told her about my brothers. How our word and loyalty is all we have when it comes to each other, but it means everything to us. Thinking about it reminds me I need to check in with guys and also give Beast a call to see how he's been doing lately. He was going to keep his ear to the ground as well as Malevolent on any new information coming through about the island. "When can we see them?"

Her saying 'we' warms me a touch, it's not like I'd planned on allowing her to go alone in the first place. There's still far too much that doesn't add up about her disappearance, and I'll be keeping close to her while I figure it out. Her father shouldn't mind, after all, he's the one who regularly calls me asking if I've heard anything about his missing daughter. She'd been gone for so long, I thought she was dead. I was harsh in the past and told him as much. He promised never to give up on her, and I certainly hope he meant it because she's alive and well and deserves everything she never had the chance to have.

"I'll call them and set everything up, okay?"

She nods vehemently, her face still tucked into my neck. She begins to give me pepper kisses over my flesh, and I jump away. I'm too invested in her, and I need to distance myself until I figure out what's going to happen with us, if anything. I need to put my guard up if she gets her life back and decides she wants nothing to do with me. It'll hurt, any amount of time away from her will, but I'll accept it if it's what she wants. I'll have no other choice. I won't be kidnapping Aura to keep her, she's already had most of her life taken away, and I refuse to add to it.

"Are you all right?" she asks, a frown marring her beautiful face as concern overtakes her features.

I nod, turning away so she won't read the apprehension on my face. "I need to shower. I have shit to do," I respond coldly and head for the master bathroom. I turn the shower faucet all the way to the left, and the moment the steam fills the stall, I step inside. The blistering water cascades over my frame as I bend my head and attempt to process everything and how my life will be changing again. I'm not ready to lose her, but in the world our parents are from, you can easily get swallowed up and become another rich, elite snob. I didn't fit in with any of them, so I turned to the MC. In their place, I gained a group of brothers I've always been able to count on.

I wash myself, lathering for far longer than necessary as I'm lost in my thoughts. I step out of the water when Aura decides to join me. Any other day, and I'd have her pushed up against the tile wall, fucking her silly. Not today. I've got other shit on my mind, like how she may meet her family and disappear from my life entirely.

Grabbing whatever I find first in my drawers, I dress and hit her father, Steven's number. I use his personal line, knowing he'll be at home, and he'll want to share this with Lucia, Aura's mother. "I found her," I say, rather than waste any more of my time with greetings and pointless pleasantries.

There's a gasp and coughing on the other end of the line. I wait while he nearly keels over before he clears his throat and apologizes. "I'm sorry. I swear I heard you say you found her. Did I hear you correctly, or is my mind playing sick tricks on me?"

"I did. She's alive, safe, and here with me."

"Is she, uh… excuse me. I'm just taken off guard. I had begun to think it wasn't possible. Us finding her, I mean. How is she?" He sounds like he's crying, and I can't blame him. I'd be doing the same thing if it were my daughter home after disappearing without a trace for so long. The entire country mourned her disappearance from their television sets, and here she is, alive, after all.

"She's fine. You can ask her yourself if you'd like?"

"No-no. I uh… wouldn't know what to say at the moment. I'm freaking out inside right now."

I can tell.

I ask, "Is there a problem?"

"Problem? No, of course not. The opposite, this is a miracle from God."

"It's something, all right. And yes, to be blunt, she's fine. She wasn't when I found her, but she is now."

"Thank you, Philip. I'll never be able to repay you for this. You name your price at any time, and it's yours."

"No, it's not necessary. I'm just happy she's home after all this time. She doesn't remember what happened to her before I found her, and at this point, we think she may never recall it."

"None of it matters now. She's home where she belongs."

Meeting her gaze across the room, I attempt to hide my emotions from her. She's dressed in one of my shirts with her hair wet and resting over her shoulder. I'll agree with him on one thing—she's definitely where she belongs. *With me.* "When would you like me to bring her to you?"

"I'll let Lucia know, and she'll plan a welcome home."

"Great," I embellish, not feeling it at all. *Let's bombard her with a party. Surely, she'll love being ambushed and overwhelmed right from the beginning,* I think sarcastically. I don't say it, but it's fucking true and unfair in every sense.

"Bring her in an evening gown, and we'll take care of everything else."

"No reporters," I state adamantly before he hangs up. "I see one of them, and I'll keep on driving."

He sighs but agrees. "Fine, no reporters. We'll make a formal statement after the welcome for any media sources and police reports. Tomorrow, shall we say six o'clock?"

"Will it be enough time for Lucia to pull together a party?"

"You just be here with my daughter, and we'll handle the rest."

"Yes, sir," I respond mockingly.

Anything for them to have a reason to throw a party, I suppose. Over the years, they've thrown lavish events several times a year. They're usually crawling with the press, so I keep as far away from them as possible. I'm damn sure I don't need my mug out there any more than it already is. Being from influential families is bad for the bounty-hunting business. It makes me, as well as anyone associated with me, a prime target for retaliation if my face is all over the front page of society pages and blogs. I hang up without another word, knowing he'll send a private security car to park outside my place. We don't need it, but I won't turn down extra protection where Aura's concerned.

I meet her penetrating stare from across the room. Hers is filled with curiosity and worry, but she needn't feel any type of way but excitement.

"You know him?"

I shrug her question off for another time. The less she realizes about me at this point, the better. "You're going back to your family tomorrow. We have to be there no later than six, and you'll need a gown."

"A gown?"

I nod. "Your family can be very formal, and at a gathering like this, they'll expect you to be in an evening dress. Think long and expensive," I clarify.

Her shoulders fall, and her hands begin to twist in the bottom fabric of my shirt she's currently claimed. "What if they aren't pleased to see me?"

"Your family loves you. Like I said before, they've been searching for you from the moment they knew you were gone. They're very wealthy, so you'll have to get used to the lifestyle they lead, but you'll never want for anything. You'll be perfect, and they'll expect very little from you, so relax."

"This makes me even more grateful I have you. You're so calm and kind. I won't know how to act or what to think around anyone else."

"You've met Briar, and you were fine. It'll be the same, you'll see," I falsely claim, not knowing if it'll end up a train wreck where I lose my shit and shoot someone. I keep that bit to myself, though, and gesture her over.

I grab my laptop and power up the screen, bringing up the search engine. "First things first, we need to find you a suitable dress to have overnighted. Blue?" I ask, remembering the dress I found her in. It was faded badly, but the shade was still blue.

"Pink, please, if it's an option."

"All colors are available. We'll order you a few, and you can choose which you like out of all of them."

Her eyes light up as a wide smile spreads across her face. She beams, and fuck my life if she isn't the most beautiful woman I've ever seen. "I've never had a few dresses before," she exclaims excitedly, and now I want to buy her a freaking closet full just to spoil her as she deserves.

I offer a grin. "Beauty, you're about to have so much more than a few dresses, you won't know what to do with them all." At this rate, she can order what she wants, and I'll foot the bill. I don't care as long as she keeps the happy expression on her face while she's here with me.

She laughs, reflecting my grin. She probably thinks I'm pulling her leg, but she has no clue she's one of the richest women on the West Coast. Let's hope she can handle all the problems that'll surely follow with it.

CHAPTER 9

HUNTER

"Mr. and Mrs..." I greet, about to introduce Steven and his wife to Aura.

He cuts me off, taking a step in our direction. He pauses directly in front of us, his eyes pinned on his now grown-up daughter. She left a toddler and came home a gorgeous, strong woman. It has to be confusing for him and his wife—I know it was for me when I first discovered her true identity. "No need for that, Philip, you know us. We're practically family," her father boasts with a wide smile.

Just great. It's exactly what I didn't want—Aura finding out I've known her father all this time, and I've been betraying her by keeping it from her. I'm an asshole, but I can't help it, nor do I want to.

They're happy, thrilled even, and I can't blame them for being overjoyed their daughter is finally home again. In their eyes, me returning with Aura has only further cemented their ideas around the two of us. My parents will be the first to back up the sentiment, I don't doubt it for a minute. I'm sure they're around here somewhere, and I'll see them before I leave.

I meet Aura's gaze, hers is stinging with betrayal, and it's pointed in my direction.

"Excuse us for just a moment," I interrupt and step a few paces away.

"You knew this entire time?" Aura accuses, hurt lacing her tone. I hate knowing I'm the one who's caused her some pain, but I had to be sure she was okay before I could bring her to her parents. I've known them my entire life, and at one point, they were sort of like an extended aunt and uncle, but Aura's disappearance changed everything for both our families.

My hands raise in defense. I'm guilty, but I have my reasons, and I don't expect her to understand them. "I had to be sure. You'd been gone for so long. I've spent my entire life looking for someone who'd become a ghost, searching for you."

Her lower lip trembles as a tear slides free. I move to wipe it away, but she turns away from my touch, not wanting to feel my fingers on her flesh. My hand falls back to my side, rejected. My fingers curl into a fist. "I had to be sure," I repeat. "I don't expect you to understand. I'll explain if you'll give me the chance, and if not, then you can continue hating me if it pleases you."

She's been blindsided, and I'm guilty of that deception as I am of far more. She doesn't need to know I was being selfish, keeping her for me alone. She'll have forever with these people, and I wanted her without all their influence. Once I realized who she was, I had to see if we could be anything without her knowing our past and if it truly was fate bringing us together again.

A figure in black steps into my peripheral vision, and instinctively, I move to Aura. I place my arm around her, clutching her to me, and murmur, "Careful with this one. I've never trusted her."

I know she catches my words as her body stiffens with each approaching step from the woman clad in all black. She's a dark stain on the party, evil surrounding every inch of her. She stands out amongst the guests in her spiked ebony shoes, dress, makeup, and hair. Even the diamonds dripping over her are the darkest shade of black available. As she pauses to stand in front of us, I rumble, "Aura, this is your aunt."

Black lips twist into a cruel grin as she stares down her sharp nose at Aura. Her words are slick and slimy as she falsely greets, "Darling! We've all missed you so. We were worried you were left for dead somewhere in a ditch."

She was hoping as much, that I don't doubt. As the next heir in line beside Aura, I wouldn't be surprised if she's the one who organized Aura's disappearance in the first place. In fact, that makes the most sense out of everything. It's an idea I've toyed with a time or two in the back of my mind, one that hasn't gone away.

"Hello, forgive me for being rude, but I don't know what your name is." Aura is the last person who should be apologizing to this vile woman. I don't interrupt as the last thing I want is to offer her aunt any pleasantries when she least deserves them. Rather, I bide my time standing behind Aura, steady as a stone for as long as she needs me to be.

"Never mind that, darling. One can't expect much when your mind is so fragile."

Bitch is an understatement when it comes to this woman. She has the nerve to be speaking down to Aura. There are plenty of us in this room tonight who can see her for what she really is. She may wear black as a silent suit of armor, but her favorite color is old-money green. She latched onto Steven and Lucia and hasn't let go of the gold chain since.

Aura offers a kind smile while standing her ground. Needless to say, I'm proud of her to see she has a backbone even when faced with a powerful adversary. "Right, what shall I call you?"

"Aunty will suffice nicely."

Luckily, we're interrupted by her father. The eager old fool doesn't want to relinquish his time with his daughter after being apart from her for so long. Living with her for the short time I have, I can understand his fondness. I don't want to give her up either.

"Why the long faces? This is a party. Everyone should be celebrating and wearing smiles. The world is right once again, and I have my daughter home with me." His face lights up as he gazes fondly at Aura, love and pride shining from him.

"Of course, Steven," I agree. "It wasn't the same without her around. We all missed her presence."

Her aunt ruins the moment by saying, "It was certainly much quieter without a clumsy toddler getting into everything."

"Aura, come with me. I need to speak with you for a moment." I tug her far enough away we won't be easily overheard by her aunt. My eagerness to get her alone is met with an icy glare. It's what I deserve, my betrayal has run deep, and I'd bet she's barely scratching the surface of her anger.

"What is it," she asks with impatience lacing her tone.

I inwardly cringe but keep any apologies to myself. I refuse to grovel for merely keeping her safe. Were my ambitions strictly selfish? One could argue they are, but I always had her safety in the forefront of my mind. "Trust me when I tell you there's something off with that woman. Don't let her get too close or ever be alone with Diana. My gut tells me she's guilty, of what, who knows. My gut never lies, so I won't begin to doubt it now. You can't trust her."

"Did your gut also tell you to lie to me about knowing who I am? All this time, Philip, you knew who my mother and father were, and you chose not to tell me. What does that say about the type of person you are, or if I can trust you at this point as well? You owe me an explanation. It's the least you can do after lying to me, after making me fall for you like a fool."

Fuck. This is worse than I thought.

I can't worry about that now, not when we're in a ballroom full of serpents. "After years of experience chasing convicts, one thing

I've learned is how to peg a criminal. No matter if they're clad in silk-lined suits, five-day-old jeans, or in this case, a black evening gown. I know that I hurt you, but it wasn't my intention. Be angry all you want but listen to me on this one last thing."

"Fine." She glances toward her father, and in my heart, I know she won't be coming home with me. Another time maybe if I'm ever so lucky to figure a way to pay penance for my betrayal, and she allows me to touch her again. I reach for her elbow testing my theory, and she proves me right when she jerks away as if she's been stung. If she only had a clue, I'm the one person here she can truly trust, betrayal or not.

Tilting my chin, I let her know she's welcome to return to her family. I don't want to keep her away from them any longer, not until she's forgiven me and we can work through this.

Making my way back with her, I shake Philip's hand. I offer a jerky nod toward the evil bitch in black and make for the exit. I hear them asking Aura about her singing and if she'll grace the guests with a song. I regret sharing the detail about her with them and should've selfishly saved it for myself. This is her first night back in her home, and yet they threw a party full of people she doesn't know and now want her on stage, playing the dutiful puppet. It's something I've never been able to stand.

My family is nearly as wealthy as Aura's, and it's one of the reasons they had so many plans for us when we became adults. Fate just so happened to intervene and cruelly steal away all options offered to us. It had to wait until we were adults, both fucked-up in our own ways before finally realigning our stars. Even with a second chance at hand, we seem to be veering in separate directions.

Needless to say, I never quite lived up to my parents' expectations, not that I give a fuck. Sure, I love them both, they were good to me growing up, but it doesn't mean I'll give up all that I am to be something I'm not. The stuffy business suit, married to Aura with four of our own little heirs running around, isn't in my cards.

As soon as I'm free from open ears and prying stares, I retrieve my cell from my pocket. There's a text from Beast, letting me know he's sending a prospect with a file for me to take a look at. Periodically, he'll do this, and I know it's his way of checking up on me. Whereas, I'll just randomly show up to make sure the fucker is still fighting his demons. I shoot him back a quick reply, grateful his new wife is keeping him too busy to dwell on the past. He deserves to be at peace.

I pull up Diablo's number. It rings once before his gruff bark comes across the line. "Yeah?"

"You find anything?"

"I did the digging as you requested, it's taken a while, but I think I found something."

"Does it involve the aunt?"

"There're rumors she hires a few low-life scum to take care of the problems she doesn't want to deal with from time to time. She believes she has the funds to buy their silence, but I hold something greater—their loyalty. The few around here who are familiar with her have admitted to helping make people disappear. Aura's name didn't come up, but I wouldn't put it past her, especially with the price Aura's head would've fetched from her family if they were to find out when she was first taken."

"One word of her potential worth as heiress to the family's botanical empire, and every cockroach with a bill to pay would've been crawling out of their holes from across the country to get a piece of her. Not only is her aunt a slimy snake, but she's also an intelligent one, which makes her all the more dangerous. It has to be her... I can feel it in my bones. She's the only person who'd benefit from her niece disappearing without a trace or a name, for that matter."

"My thoughts exactly. She needs to be thoroughly questioned. What will you do?"

"It'll have to wait. I can't talk about it right now. Aura is surrounded by the rest of her family, so I have to believe they're capable of keeping her safe as an adult."

"And if they aren't? If she's hurt under their watch?"

"There's only one true killer in town, and it's me. They'll learn as much the hard way, should they push me."

"It will be their funerals, brother. I've got your back, always."

"Appreciate it and for you passing along the information."

"No problem. I'll hit you up if I hear anything else."

"Sounds good. Later." I hang up and tuck my phone away.

As I'm stepping toward the bathroom, Aura's aunt enters the foyer. I quickly duck around the nearest corner, so she misses me. I'm close enough to hear anything going on and also peek around for a visual if needed.

"I told you she was back!" she vehemently whispers toward the man. I've never seen him before, but he could be part of the staff. "I thought it was a phony, but one look at her, and there's not a doubt in my mind she's my brother's child. You *have* to do something. We'll get nothing if she's alive. I told you when she was a baby, and you promised to deal with it. All this time I believed she was dead, so imagine my surprise when I discovered that was never the case! I swear I'm surrounded by incompetent idiots."

His hands go up, attempting to calm the snarling terror of a woman. "I took care of it and gave her away to a skin trader. It wasn't only her but also three other little bitches. He was selling them all off to some high-scale bidder. How was I supposed to know your niece would show up unharmed?"

"This isn't good. This can't be happening. She has to disappear again, and this time for good."

"What are you saying?" he asks, and she replies bluntly.

"Kill her."

My hands begin to shake, so I curl them into fists. Now's not the time to go out half-cocked and declare them guilty. Of course, they are, I just heard them talking, but I need a plan first. Rich people don't just go down without some sort of a fight. Usually, it's the opposite, and they twist the trouble around to bring the turmoil to you tenfold.

My heart's thundering in my chest so loudly it's hard to hear anything at all for a beat. I breathe deeply, attempting to still my thoughts and slow my pulse. I've done this too many times to count, lay and wait for my chance to pounce. Lord, will I ever with these two? I only need the perfect chance to come along.

Pulling my phone out again, I hit the record feature. I'm sure it's too far away to pick up their voices, but it's still a shot I don't plan to waste.

"Grab her tonight. We don't have any time to waste," Diana orders, and the guy dips his head in submission, ready to do her dirty work.

"If there's an opportunity to grab her, I will," he promises. Little does he know I won't ever allow it to come to fruition. I'll get her to safety as soon as they end this secretive meeting of theirs.

"Make one if you have to, I don't care. Just get it taken care of. This is all your fault. We'd never be in this mess if you'd killed her already."

"I said I'll handle it."

"You better," she hisses, sounding more serpent than human. It wouldn't surprise me if she was some vile creature from hell, come to steal the joy from others.

Evil psychotic bitch.

I'm too focused on the pair that I don't pay my phone any attention. My hand grows sweaty with my nerves and anger, so the cell falls from my grip. I lunge forward, attempting to catch the small rectangle before it lands, but it's no use. It clamors to the ground with a 'thwack' sound, and with it, I glance toward the couple only to realize my hiding spot has been exposed.

The guy rushes at me unexpectedly, hitting my stomach full force. We fall to the floor, him having the upper hand from catching me off guard. I've been doing this for far too long, though, and quickly recover enough to climb on top and rain fists below. I bust his face up, blood going everywhere. Once I start, I don't anticipate stopping with this guy. I was willing to formulate a plan to catch the two in the act of messing with Aura, but I'll take killing him with my bare hands as an option as well.

"You, stupid boy, you never know when to keep your nose out of other people's business." I hear beside me before shocks overtake my body. I can feel where the metal prongs from her taser are latched on to me, but the unit is far too strong for me to fight it completely. All I can do is freeze my muscles up and jolt around on the floor while she pumps enough amps in me to fry my brain and reflexes until tomorrow. Drool spills from my mouth like a weak punk as I continue to shake, then a sharp crack to the back of my head has everything fading to complete blackness around me.

I'm fucked.

CHAPTER 10

AURA

Hunter left without me. The thought hits me repeatedly while I stand staring off into space, uncertain of what I should be doing. I can't believe he's gone without even a backward glance.

I've said hello to so many people and thanked them for coming that it's turned into an automatic response at this point. If I've hurt their feelings or upset them otherwise, I can't bring myself to care. I don't know any of them, even if a few do state they knew me as a child. I was a toddler when I went missing, so surely, they can't expect me to remember any of them. I struggled just thinking of my parents at times on the island, I even cried occasionally because I felt like they were fading from my memory.

"How are you holding up, my sweet girl?" my father asks as he moves to stand beside me.

What would he say if I told him I'm a bit heartbroken, confused, and tired? Mix those three, and I'm the trifecta of an emotional woman searching for where things went wrong when they've merely just begun. "I'm fine," I reply instead, feeling anything but the sort.

Hunter

I should be happy right now, thrilled even. I've been reunited with the loving family I always wondered about. I wasn't told I'd been kidnapped from my family. My friends always said we ended up lost, and it was their job to look after me. I know I'm going to have to give my parents and the authorities details of my disappearance and the years leading up to now. It doesn't bother me much, only the possibility of Laura, Luna, and Mary getting in trouble because of everything. They didn't have anything to do with my disappearance, and I won't believe otherwise no matter what anyone says differently.

Hunter hasn't found any new information on them, so he told me to think of them as safe and underground. He's gone now, though, so it's hard for me to take whatever he's said as solid advice. Sure, I want to believe him, but I'm torn because clearly, I've been wrong about his character as well. I figured he'd remain with me the entire night, perhaps even a sleepover at my parents' house tonight. The place is certainly large enough to house a small army should they decide to. It's too large for me to feel comfortable, and the longer I remain, the more I want to return to Hunter's place. His is a decent size, too, but not nearly this lavish and untouched.

The welcome-home party my parents have organized for me is in their private ballroom. It sounds ostentatious, but the space is truly wonderful and decorated with lovely, scented flowers. I don't know if Hunter told them about my adoration for the outdoors, but it's clear they went to the trouble to incorporate one of my favorite things.

Something tells me they wouldn't be quite as thrilled or understanding if I told them I'd rather sleep outside in nature than alone under their massive roof. I don't want to offend them or anything, but a piece of me feels as if I've only just met them. Hunter is what I know, who I feel safe and content with even if he did hurt me with his betrayal.

I don't have a way to reach him. Would he want to hear from

me after everything that's happened? "Do you have a phone I can call Hunter on? As well as his phone number?"

"Who, my dear?" my mother asks, meeting my gaze.

"Hunter," I begin, and she waves me off.

"Oh, Philip. Yes, of course, we have a phone you can use. Your father will have his number, but don't bother the boy. He's done so much for us already."

He's a far cry from any boy I've ever imagined, but I don't argue. I don't want to rock the boat with them already. "Where can I sleep?" I ask instead of demanding she call Hunter and have him come pick me back up like I want. I need to give my family a chance before bolting out of here on a whim.

"Come on, beautiful. I'll take you to your princess suite."

I like pink, but something tells me I'm not ready for what she's about to show me. I follow her up the long staircase and then to the right when she heads in a direction with only two doors. There are massive double doors at the very end and a single door off toward the middle of the hallway. She pauses long enough to open the single door and flick on a light. My curiosity gets the better of me, and I peek my head in without being invited. I draw in a stunned breath at what I discover—white and light blush everywhere. It's so stunning it brings tears to my eyes. "This is mine?"

She nods, her gaze growing watery as well. "Yes, this was your room as an infant and toddler. The doors at the end of the hall were always meant for you as well, but you never got to use them." Tears break free, trailing over her cheeks. She pulls me in for a hug on a burst of emotion, and I wind my arms around her tightly. This is the welcome I was hoping for, not the big party downstairs where I felt on display for everyone I don't ever remember meeting.

"It's so… so peaceful," I say, trying to think of the right word to describe it properly. "I thought I'd remembered it, but it must've been another room, perhaps." My stare flicks over the warm twinkle lights, the fluffy ivory ottoman-style chairs, and a small princess bed. There's a golden crown and sheer, filmy fabric at the top as well, making it feel straight out of a fairy tale.

The skin around her eyes crinkles as she tilts her head and asks, "What room do you recall?"

"I remember being in a giant bed, laying between you and father as he read me stories."

Her hand goes to cover her mouth as sobs begin to rip free. I pull her to me again, not sure why she's so upset or what to do to stop it. Was it a bad memory? It's always been a favorite of mine. I hold her while her shoulders shake, not sure how else to comfort her. I feel for her, I really do, but what did I say?

Eventually, she pulls back, her palms moving to warm my cheeks as she meets my gaze. "I can't believe you remember your father reading. He made sure to tell you a new story every night before you went to sleep. You were so insistent after a while, you refused to sleep until you heard one. At some point when he was on business, he'd read to you over the phone." She offers a kind smile. "I thought you'd forget."

I shake my head. "Never." It also explains why Mary told me stories so much. I probably drove her crazy as a child.

She releases me, leaving the door and light on in my old bedroom to head for the end of the hallway. "I hope you love this space but feel free to do whatever you want with it. This is your home, and you're welcome to change anything." She offers an excited smile as she opens both doors, and the light comes on automatically.

I follow her inside, my mouth gaping at the magnificent features. The ceiling alone is remarkable. It's filled with unique tiles and gold trim. In the middle is a massive mural filled with angels and flowers. There are so many different kinds—roses, chrysanthemums, orchids, lilies, hydrangea—too many varieties for me to process at once. "Wow, this is stunning." My gaze falls to the rest of the space, and I find myself wondering what Hunter would look like in here. His presence is consuming, so much so I bet it'd feel remarkably smaller in here with him inside.

"I'm glad you like it. I put a lot of thought into it over the years. If you ever made your way home back to us, I wanted to make sure you had something nice waiting for you."

"I lived in a place made from trees and brush. The floor was dirt." I don't know why I share as much with her, perhaps to set her at ease. I never minded living on the island—for me, it was almost all I knew. I'm sure it was hard at first, but I was a toddler. I didn't have any choice but to adapt and overcome any obstacle we faced. I'm grateful to Laura, Luna, and Mary for all they've done for me. "I didn't know this is where I truly came from. I believed most of my memories I'd made up at some point or embellished them."

My mother shakes her head. "No, you're the heir to our botanical company."

"Do you mean flowers or something different?"

"Flowers, yes. The many blooms downstairs today came from one of our several farms. We have all types from upscale boutiques to well-known chain stores selling our products. Of course, it's not only flowers, but we also sell a variety of products for them as well. Your father has become quite famous for his eye for quality. Over the years, your father not only grew the empire, but he also trades stocks and such. He's made us very wealthy, and it's all yours as well."

"I didn't work for this."

"No, but we did it to offer our family a good life. We want to share it with you."

I offer her a kind smile. She has a good heart and is genuine—I can read it on her easily. Earlier at the party, she and my father seemed so different, maybe they were acting a certain way because of all the people around us, but I could be wrong. "What about my aunt?"

Her lips briefly tip downward. She sighs and glances me over. She carefully takes my hand and pulls me toward my bed with a lace paisley coverlet that's more delicate than anything I've ever owned. I'm supposed to sleep with it, which both excites and terrifies me. "Diana is your father's sister. She's always been jealous, I suppose. It became more pronounced when you were born, but she changed once you were kidnapped. She's stepped up and hired many private investigators to try to find you for us."

"And Hunter?"

She grins. "Always back to him... I shouldn't be surprised. He's been stuck to your side since you were born. He was your own little soldier, always looking out for you when you were tiny. We thought it fate, you and he intertwined throughout your lives, and perhaps it'd blossom into something more. Unfortunately, when you disappeared, those hopes and dreams went along with your absence. I couldn't cope day to day for many years. My friendship with his mother suffered terribly. His father, Henry, and yours are still good friends, though."

"He's a decent guy, though?" I want her to confirm. I already know what I think of him, but I need to hear it come from my mother as well. I have to learn to re-trust my instincts, but Hunter has thrown me all off track with him leaving abruptly and withholding important information.

"He's had his hand in a bit of trouble from time to time. He's toed the line between good and evil. Overall, however, yes, I'd say that young man is good. His heart is pure, and in the end, that's where it truly matters the most with love."

I dip my head, silently agreeing with her. Talking about him only makes me miss him more and wonder all over again what I did to make him leave so suddenly. Men are confusing, I'm learning as much already.

My mother lets the subject drop for now, going back to the latter. "Speaking of your aunt. She has a room here, or rather, a wing. She comes and goes as she pleases, so don't be surprised if you see her around. She may be moody at times, but she's harmless overall. Don't let her push you around if she should try. Stand up for yourself, and she'll back off. I had to do the same many years ago when I started dating your father."

"What general direction is hers in so I can stay far out of her way?"

"Hmm." She shakes her head. "You're our main priority. Don't worry for a minute about being in her way, you go wherever you desire. The world is at your fingertips, and we'll do whatever we can to make sure your happiness is at the forefront. We want you to succeed and live a fulfilled life."

"I appreciate it. Thank you for your understanding and kindness about it all."

She waves me off. "Of course, my beauty. Besides, your aunt is usually in the lower level, underneath the house. There's the garage and another level as well. Your father had a lab amongst other rooms built down there when he designed this house. I don't know what she fills her days in within the dreary space, but it certainly involves her wearing a lot of black." She ends it with a soft melodic laugh.

It's contagious, and I find myself giggling along with her. "Underground lair, noted. I'll stick to above ground." Hopefully, it's enough not to have any more run-ins with the wretched woman. You wouldn't think she'd act so rudely by looking at her. She's quite stunning in her own Medusa sort of way.

She smiles widely, her hand gently patting my cheek. She stands, gliding toward another door tucked in the corner of the room. She opens the door, and a light immediately flips on automatically. It'll take me some time to get used to the feature and so much space, no doubt. "This is your closet. I had the staff run out today and pick up some satin and silk pajamas. There are nightgowns, shorts, pants, robes, slippers, and anything else your heart could desire tonight. We'll go shopping soon, perhaps take a trip to Paris and make a weekend of it. I love their selections every time we visit. So much variety to choose from you don't find here."

I smile with a quick nod. The thought of jetting to another country is exciting but also kind of terrifying since I've just met her after being gone most of my life. I'd probably feel comfortable if a certain broody biker were with us, and don't get me started about having everything my heart desires tonight. If my mother knew I wanted the biker in my bed, naked, she'd probably pass out. While I'm thinking about health, I remember what Hunter told me about when he found me. Probably best to ask my mother as she'd be the one to know about my medical history. "Oh, um, am I allergic to anything?"

"Hmm. Foods or bugs or something else?"

"Anything you're aware of, especially plants."

She frowns for a second before her face lights with an answer, and she holds a finger up. "Yes, as a matter of a fact, you are. Iodine, betadine, and poison sumac. Poison sumac is found in swamps, wetlands, pinewoods, and hardwood forests. It has multiple forms growing as a shrub or small tree that can get as tall as twenty-five feet or so. It looks completely harmless, but it can be deadly to you. I'll show you pictures tomorrow, so you're well aware of what it is. I'll also make sure it's destroyed from any of our properties. I won't have you touching it accidentally."

"Thank you. I appreciate everything," I say again, but I feel like I can't tell her enough.

"I know you do, my sweet girl. Not a girl anymore, though, I suppose." She sniffles, getting emotional. "You're such an amazing woman already, I can hardly wait to get to know you. Now, get some rest. We have lots of catching up to do. Sleep as long as you need to. You're safe here in a house full of people who love you."

"Good night, please tell my father for me."

"I will. I apologize on his behalf. He's much more emotional today than he has been in quite a long time. He needs to gain his bearings. After a few days, he'll be around more and most likely peppering you with questions. He'll want to know absolutely everything about you. Your father has always adored you with everything he is." She leaves me with the parting thought, closing the bedroom door behind her.

As soon as I'm alone, I head for the closet, lose the constrictive evening gown for a soft night dress in pale blue. It reminds me of my old dress. It may have been tattered and torn, but it was mine. I move to the massive windows at the far side of the room and discover a door leading outside to a balcony. I open them all, breathing in the cool night air deeply.

Rather than sleep in the lavish bed, I grab the blankets and place them next to the windows and door. Laying down, I curl up on my side to stare out into the darkness. I find the stars, the same dim lights I've watched many nights while falling asleep. This time, I don't wonder what's out there past our tiny hut, but rather, if Hunter is gazing at them as well.

CHAPTER 11

HUNTER

The first thing I notice waking up is it doesn't sound like it should. My brain's a bit foggy with confusion, and I'm disoriented. Rather than peel my lids back, I take a few brief moments to breathe deeply and work to get my thoughts in order. I remember being at the welcome party with Aura, and then afterward, my mind trails off as bits and pieces begin clicking into place.

Fuck. This isn't good at all.

With a deep exhale, I open my eyes. I'm already aware I won't like what I find waiting for me, and I'm right. My hands, along with the rest of my body, are tied securely. Apparently, a satanist bound my ass up as they wrapped my entire frame in the offending rope. I wiggle, testing the strength and am pinched in random spots. This is bullshit, and everything inside me wants to pop a fuse and lose my shit. The urge to roar and bellow profanities rides my shoulders heavily, but I refrain. Throwing a tantrum will get me nowhere, no matter how much satisfaction it may momentarily bring. I also need to reserve my energy. I don't know what I'm in for with what went down.

Think. I need to be smart about this.

The psycho bitch plans to kill Aura, and I have no idea what sort of timeframe she's working with. Whatever I do, I need a plan and one that'll get me out of here quickly. I have to get to Aura. I'll never forgive myself if something happens to her. After all this time, the least she deserves are new hurdles to leap over in life. I can't believe I promised to protect her, and I've already failed in the first step.

I take in my surroundings, searching for anything I may be able to use. I'm lying on an inky, thick exercise type of mat that fills up a generous portion in the corner of the main room. There are a few hallways veering off from this room—I'm assuming that's what they are anyway. There's no telling what all is down here with me or where I'm at in general. The endless possibilities have me grinding my molars as I continue to catalog everything with dread.

Someone must've seen something at the party—they had to. I know for certain that Steven and Lucia have cameras all over their massive mansion. Surely, they're looking for me by now. The possibility of this psychotic bitch having further reach comes slithering into the back of my mind like a suffocating fog.

The reality of my situation is I'm at her mercy and have no clue just how far her deception carries. For all I know, she could have several on staff working for her—the man I saw earlier with her was one I've deduced. This is even worse than I imagined. I thought she was merely a pest with good connections in the past, but clearly, I've underestimated her. It doesn't help she's Steven's sister, and he most likely trusts her blindly. It'll end up getting him and Lucia killed as well, I don't doubt as much for even a second.

Diana obviously wants whatever she can get her hands on, and she isn't afraid to take what she wants by force if necessary. I'd believed she was only after Aura's spot as heir to the botanical throne, but now I have a feeling it's much more. I'm watching her across the room on a computer when she spins and finally notices

I've come to. I'm grouchy and groggy, but I won't let her know as much. As far as she's concerned, I'm a fucking spring chicken, waiting to pounce.

"Ah, the nosey nuisance has finally awoken. You've been a thorn in my side for far too long. You're here until I decide what's to become of you. Anger me, and I'll have you drowned," she promises, coming close enough I could spit on her. I've never wanted to kill a woman before, but she's quickly becoming the first. I'd even settle for torture and jail time so long as she's adequately punished for her crimes.

"Drown me, and my club comes for your head. They'll dice you and your accomplices up while you each watch, screaming in pain."

Her throaty tone fills the room with her evil cackle. The sound creeps me out, but I manage to suppress the shudder wanting to surface. "No one would ever expect me of hurting someone, let alone you. There's no personal link between us, so you can disappear without a blink in my direction."

"You're wrong. I've had my brothers quietly up your ass so far they know what time you take a shit. Come at me or Aura, and you're as good as tortured, then rotting in prison. Hurt us and you'll meet certain death, I'll make sure of it."

Wearing a malicious grin, she strides toward me with purpose. The room echoes with the crack of her palm meeting my flesh. I put her in for a dainty bitch, but she knows how to slap. She holds her hands up and spins, mocking me. "Oh, whatever will happen to me now?" Her mouth drops into a scowl as she nastily snarls, "Nothing. And it never will."

With a chuckle, I shake my head. "Not only are you a dumbass, but you hit like one too." My spit lands on her face, which isn't the easiest feat, I'll have you know, laying on the ground tied up as I am. I'm met with a swift kick in retaliation. Her small foot slams into my stomach with enough force, I gasp for breath.

"You fool. Aura's right upstairs, and I'll have her down here next to you faster than you can count to twenty. I already have everything planned, so you better not push me."

Ah, but it worked. I've pissed her off enough, she coughed up information she wouldn't have otherwise been so forthcoming with. It may not be the smartest move, getting myself injured in the process, but I had to do something I knew would work. Now, I know I'm still in the mansion, and Aura's safe for the moment. In the meantime, I need to figure a way out of this place.

I'm not lying about my brothers looking into possible leads as to who took Aura, but they aren't involved as deeply as I stated. I'm an idiot for not including them more, or there'd be a decent chance they would be on their way here by now. I wiggle around, watching as Aura's sadistic aunt leaves the room without me knowing where she's going. I don't feel anything in my pockets, can't say I'm surprised, though. There's not much room for hiding anything in a pair of damn dress slacks. My phone's missing as well, so there's no way I can attempt to alert my brothers. Not like I could anyhow since I'm fucking tied up. I'm basically screwed unless I can manage to get these ropes loose somehow.

I lay waiting, impatient and attempting to keep track of time, as well as any noises I might pick up. There are not many, and it's not a good sign. I'm expecting a security guard or other staff to show up at some point, but it never happens. Essentially, I gain nothing I can use and only manage to get more confused about how long I've been down here. It would have been easier if I wasn't knocked unconscious because I have no idea how long it took me to come to. I'm assuming I slept through the night because of Diana's recent wardrobe change. Being a bounty hunter, I've always tried to take in the smaller details people overlook, as you never know when something may come in handy later.

Eventually, I doze off again. I try to fight it, but it's no use. I've most likely gotten a mild concussion from the crack to my head. It's not the first time, but it won't make my escape any easier on me either.

I wake up again, this time to voices talking in hushed tones. I keep my eyes closed, managing to make out Aura's Aunt Diana and her henchman's voices.

"I'm telling you... this *will* work. I overheard Lucia and Aura talking last night. She's deathly allergic to this type of plant. It's very poisonous to certain people."

"But it's only a few leaves," the idiot argues, and I chance a glance, wanting to see what they're up to.

They're not paying attention to me, so I openly stare. On the screen against the far wall is a plant called poison sumac, and it has several pictures along with the plant's properties. I glare at it for a while, memorizing the images. If I could go back to the spot I found Aura, I'd bet money the poison sumac is around there somewhere and it made her ill. I already know what happens to her if she's exposed enough, and I doubt she has any clue what it looks like. Knowing her, she'll touch it and probably even sing to the deadly thing before it ever hits her there's a lick of danger involved. The green thumb of hers will be her death if she's not cautious around Diana.

"What are we doing with him?" He nods my way, and they both glance at me, noticing I'm awake. Hopefully, it doesn't make them stop discussing their plan. I need as much intel as I can possibly gather at this point.

Diana shrugs. "Once Aura's swollen up and dead, bury them together. They can finally have one another." She laughs cruelly, probably hoping to get a response out of me.

I refuse to give her what she wants, so I stare blankly, shutting off my outward emotions. Inside, however, I'm a gnarled mess of worry and regret. I shouldn't have pushed Aura away once I decided it was time for her parents to finally learn about her existence. It may have been done in self-preservation, but it was the wrong thing to do. Aura would be safe and happy right now if I'd stuck to her side as I'd wanted. Instead, I was a stubborn ass, and now we're both in danger with no one to help save us. If she dies because of me, it'll eat me alive inside.

"What did she ever do to warrant your hate?" I finally ask, at my wit's end of not knowing. Aura is the kindest woman I've ever met, so I find it incredibly hard to imagine anyone with hate directed in her direction.

"She was born," Diana replies without missing a beat. "I was supposed to be my brother's heir, not her. Now she'll disappear forever, and the title will go back to me, where it should've stayed all along. Steven's betrayal will not go unpunished."

"He betrayed you how?" This is the first time I'm hearing anything of the sort.

"Shut up!" Her goon orders, but Diana answers my question anyway. She loves being in the spotlight, always has.

"He betrayed me by getting rid of me at the company once Aura was born. He no longer needed me as his heir since she was around. Lucia's far too rich to need any of Steven's money, so why shouldn't I get it? I'm family, too, but everyone seems to forget that simple fact whenever it's convenient. Well, now it's my turn to get rid of the inconvenience."

I shake my head as much as the floor allows. "Greed. This is all because you want Steven's money and not have to work for it. You really are a piece of shit."

She fumes at my words—she can't seem to handle the truth. Not that many psychopaths can, but I was expecting a little bit more from the woman who orchestrated her niece's kidnapping and disappearance. "You know nothing, black sheep. A lot of good being away from your family has done you, even they won't care if you're gone."

With a careless shrug, I roll my eyes. I don't give a fuck what she thinks and attempting to bring it on a personal level toward me will only make me fight harder to come out on top of this situation.

"Not that it's any of your business, but my family loves me all the same. I didn't choose their path, but it doesn't mean they aren't supportive of the one I'm on. Being the black sheep only means I understand you better than you'll ever admit. Don't get too cocky, you keep forgetting I'm in an MC. Whether my parents look for me or not, my club brothers will, and they're much more ruthless than my own blood. I hope you've got a dark hole somewhere to crawl in and hide 'cause you'll damn sure need it." I keep talking shit, hoping it'll strike a chord with Diana and her lackey. I'm not sure anything will happen, but I talk a good game, so hopefully, something I say will have them eventually shitting their pants and leaving Aura alone.

"You know my brothers love Aura. She's the little sister they never had, and brothers are protective. I can't wait to see what they do with you two from threatening her safety alone." Aura's only met Briar for the most part. She's seen my other brothers stop by briefly for a few words, but it's about as far as their relationships have gone. If I get out of here alive, their knowledge will be one of the first things I change. I'll properly introduce Aura as my girl if she'll have me, and they can form their own opinions of her. I've been selfish, hogging Aura all to myself, but it'll stop due to her safety.

"Don't listen to anything he says," she orders the guy who's busily scowling in my direction. He seems great, the real friendly sort. I see why he's so attracted to Diana, like attracts like, and they're both despicable.

To fuck with him a bit, I wink and blow him air kisses. He looks like the type who can't handle confrontation or taunting well. "Come here, big boy, let me dot your other eye for you. I'll make 'em match, you weak little bitch."

"Fuck you!" He loses it and screams with rage.

"Shh!" Diana warns. "Enough. I won't tolerate filth from you. I told you to ignore Philip, and I mean it. I'll let you know when the time is right to kill him too. You'll exact your contempt for him then and no sooner. Now, go find out my niece's schedule so we can get this over with. I want her dead and buried before my brother has a chance to alter the will again."

"I'll handle it."

"You better. Make sure no one suspects anything. Think flawless, just how I like my diamonds."

He nods submissively and strides for the doorway.

"You still have time to change your mind," I offer, aware it'll most likely do me no good, but it's worth a shot anyhow.

She hums, flashing me an amused glance. "I can always change my mind. No one has the power to dictate otherwise."

I nod. "Exactly. You're not too deep right now, so things in motion can be changed. You can let me go and not deal with the consequences of holding me captive." It's a load of bullshit, but I go with it anyhow. Whether this woman lets me go or not, I'm slitting her throat the first chance I get. The world deserves to be purged of filth like her. If only I were closer to my knife. I glance longingly at it once Diana turns away from me again.

"You're a funny one, thinking you can talk me into allowing you to go free. Not happening, you'll die right along with my niece."

She couldn't be further from the truth. I'll figure something out to warn Aura, even if I have to die trying.

CHAPTER 12

AURA

"Hmm." The woman taking my measurements makes the distinctive sound again for the third time. I'm ready to demand she tell me exactly what it means, but with my mother beside me, smiling pleasantly, it's held me back from voicing my frustrations with this entire process.

"I don't need anything tailored. I can try something on and be fine with whatever we find," I murmur, not wanting anyone to go out of their way. Clothes are only meant to help shield you from the weather, nothing more. My mother insisted I needed my items tailored, but I had no clue what it even meant until she elaborated, and it made me feel foolish for asking.

"With these hips, you'll have to be measured, or nothing will fit properly," the woman insists, and I flash a frustrated glance at my mother. I'm pretty sure her comment was rude, but I don't know what to say in response.

She smiles warmly. "Take it as a compliment, my dear. Women are paying small fortunes to have your shape."

"Then why aren't there clothes already made that'll fit me?"

"Because you're blessed with these attributes, and unfortunately, most of us aren't. You have the waist of an eight, along with hips and behind of a fourteen. Philip was smart getting you a stretchy fabric for your evening gown as it encased all your gorgeous curves perfectly. I'm also not surprised he followed you around for most of the night, glowering at every man who glanced in your direction."

"Mm-hmm," the tailor nods, poking me in random places. "You've never had implants? For certain, I thought you had them in your behind."

My mother gasps. "Matilda, how dare you ask my daughter such a question. Of course, she's natural, and she's beautiful the way she is. Anyone claiming differently is doing it purely out of jealousy, and you're not to believe a word they spew."

Matilda shrugs the reprimand off. "I see them so frequently now, it's not as uncommon as you think. You weren't fibbing about many women paying for them to look like Aura."

I'm so lost with this conversation, and I have no idea how to respond. Rather, my thoughts snag on what she's mentioned about Hunter. "I didn't notice Hunter glaring at any men around us at the party," I point out, and my mother laughs.

"Trust me, he was making it loud and clear for anyone of the male anatomy to keep their distance. Why does he have you calling him Hunter? You shouldn't pay any mind to those silly nicknames. The boy has a respectable name and should use it, especially in public."

"Have you or my father heard from him?"

My mom flashes a glance at the tailor, probably judging how much she's invested eavesdropping in on my question. My mother warned me we couldn't discuss some things in public, but she never told me what exactly those touchy items were.

"Can I borrow your phone? I'd like to speak to him, please."

"Certainly, but keep it brief, my dear," she replies, her tone laced with warning. I've barely been home for two days, and I've already begun to figure my mother out. I wish I could say the same for my father, but so far, he's kept his distance. Tonight's supposed to be different, though. My mother promises he'll be around for dinner this evening. Hence, the shopping trip—I had nothing suitable to wear, according to her.

She holds the device out to me, and I stare at it. I learned how to use the phone at the house, but this one is completely different, and I haven't the faintest clue where to start with it. "Would you mind?" I ask, gesturing to the phone.

My lack of use registers in her gaze, and she nods, offering me a soft look. I don't know what exactly it means, but I have a feeling she feels sorry for me. The last thing I want is anyone's pity. I wasn't traumatized while I was away, simply living a different type of life. I wish everyone understood as much. I like to believe Hunter gets it—he's never once looked at me like I was lacking anything. He respects me, and in return, I offer him the same.

My mother fusses with her fancy phone for a minute or so, then hands it over. I place the receiver to my ear and listen as it rings. Eventually, his voice message comes on. I got the same recording last time, and it makes me frown. I don't know what I should think or how I feel about him cutting off all contact with me. It's not like Hunter. He would've gone ballistic if I'd lost touch with him somehow, and now he completely goes cold toward me? I'm not buying it one bit.

"What is it? Did you not reach him?" she asks as I hand the phone over.

I shake my head, my frown turning severe. "It doesn't seem right."

"Maybe he needs some space. It's common for men, especially his age."

"No," I argue. "I may have just come home, but I've been with him long enough to know this isn't normal. Something isn't right. I can feel it here." I place my palm against my abdomen.

My stomach keeps twisting and turning. I thought it was nerves for this shopping trip, but it can't be the case. I never denied my senses on the island, and now I find myself doing exactly that here. Haven't I learned by now it's what obviously kept me alive and well for so long? I was running from something. I still can't remember what before I got sick and nearly died. If I hadn't been on the move, I know I would've still been fine.

With a jerky nod, she keeps her phone out. "All right, I trust your instinct."

"What are you going to do?"

"I'm calling your father and letting him know we need the location of your young man."

I sigh with relief. "Thank you."

"It's what mothers do," she reasons and tucks a lock of my hair behind my ear. It fell from my braid when we were outside, and the wind blew it around. I eagerly watch her while she speaks to my father, eavesdropping as much as possible. She hangs up and nods. "It's taken care of. Now please pick out some fabrics and styles you like."

With a shaky smile, I give in and gesture to random items. I pick multiple shades of pinks and blues, as they've always been my favorite colors. I don't know how I know as much, but I just do. I select a rich chocolate leather jacket as well as an ebony-colored one, thinking Hunter may like me in them. My mother helps me with matching boots and grabs several short and tall pairs, along with some stretchy jeans the tailor swears will fit me.

By the time we're finished, the bags have been packed up and set off to the side. The store will deliver them along with a few rush items my mother's having altered for me today. I don't know what the hurry is since I don't have anywhere to go or anything to do. I took the jeans and short booties to wear for dinner tonight. I was too excited to have them immediately to leave them for delivery.

I wish Hunter would come back and take me with him, even for a short time, but I don't think it'll happen. I fondly caress the black leather of the jacket I picked out, and I can't get over how smooth the texture is. I wore it out of the store just in case Hunter miraculously shows up. I want to see his reaction to me having something similar to his. I've daydreamed about riding his motorcycle with him before, and the thoughts come to me now as well. The soft leather jacket would be perfect for a ride in the wind.

"Get your head out of the clouds, Aura," my mother teases, wearing a knowing smile. "Go put your new clothes on, and then meet me in the kitchen so I can see how they look."

"Okay." I offer a grin and jog up the stairs toward my room. I take the time needed to properly freshen up, releasing my messy hair to re-braid the long strands. I do it twice, weaving the hair until I eventually get it styled how I want it. Finding a plain t-shirt in my closet meant for sleeping, I decide to pair it with my outfit. It's not as fancy as my parents prefer to dress, but it's okay. This style seems to fit me, and I'm happy to have found something.

Glancing in the mirror, I take in the new items from top to bottom. My casual shirt fits a touch snugly around my breasts the way I like, so I tuck in the looser bottom into the back of my jeans. With a stylish leather jacket on top, jeans hugging my hips like a second skin, and the cute black leather booties to finish it off, I'm pleasantly surprised. I didn't think much of clothes before, but this outfit suits me. I love it enough to know it's a favorite for now and in the future. My hair back with wisps framing my face, cheeks flushed, and lip gloss finish off my new look.

I quietly make my way down the stairs, stuck in my head over Hunter. I shouldn't care as much as I do, but I can't seem to stop and turn the thoughts off. Where is he anyway? He should've contacted me by now. I wish I knew how to get ahold of some of his friends. I have a feeling they'd know how to reach him.

I nearly run smack into my aunt. "Oh! Diana. Your startled me."

Her lips quirk into a smile. Her expression's not friendly in the slightest, but it never is. She radiates hostility, and it sends my nerves on edge. She's the one person Hunter told me to watch out for, and as much as I don't want to heed his warning, I will. He's always kept me safe, so I'll take his word where she's concerned.

"Well, look at you." Her gaze rakes over me. "Someone's been playing dress-up with their daddy's credit card. How convenient."

My mouth pops open, unsure of how to respond. She almost seems angry about me wearing new clothes. It's not like I was out spending until I drained my family's bank accounts. I was simply getting clothes since I don't have many. Or any, really. I wore Hunter's while I stayed with him, and since I've been here, I've worn what was in my closet from my mother.

"Thank you for noticing. Diana, is it?" I ask, although I know exactly who she is. I drop the aunt title in a tiny defiant form of disrespect. I'm not outright rude like she is—I've never been that way before. My friends never spoke to me with such bitterness, so I never did in return either.

"Yes, I'm your aunt. From your father's side, of course. The smart genes run on our side of the family."

"I don't care for what you're implying." I stand to my full height, meeting her stare head-on.

"Good thing your thoughts and opinions aren't relevant to me then." She shrugs and walks off without another word.

I'm scowling by the time I make it to the kitchen.

"Not a fan of the fit?" my mother asks as soon as she reads my expression.

I drop the irritation and offer up a small smile. I need to be grateful she spent the day with me getting me what I needed. "I love them, thank you. It's quite generous of you and father. I hope I'm not imposing."

Her smile screws up into confusion. "What are you talking about? Of course, you're not imposing, you belong here. This is your home, and we want you here and love you."

"It's just with Father and now Diana—"

She cuts me off. "Your father will be at dinner, he promised me already. He was taking care of the media, security, and catching his breath after finally having his little girl back where she belongs. He was overwhelmed. When he last saw you, you came up to his thigh, and now you're this beautiful lady. As for Diana, well, you'll learn to ignore her ugliness. She may have flawless skin and a slight frame, but karma will catch up with her eventually. She's been extra testy lately. Don't pay her any mind, and it'll settle itself. You'll see."

"What's this I hear? Problems so soon?" my father asks, entering the kitchen. He takes me in, offers me a wide smile, and pulls me in for a hug. He holds me for a beat, then two and three. Long enough to make me choke up with emotion. I've wanted him to hug me and hold me like this from the moment Hunter contacted him.

"It's nothing. I'm grateful to be here, and for the generosity you've both shown me."

"What's mine is yours. You'll learn as much. As for Diana, she has mood spells. Give her a little time. If she doesn't warm to you, I'll ask her to stay in her city apartment."

"I don't want to put her out any. I'm sure it'll get better," I state without much conviction. It's hard to be positive about someone who acts the way she does.

My mother's brow pops up, reading my uncertainty. "No, don't worry about her. She's an adult with a pampered life, and you've been surviving in the wild."

I clear my throat. "Ugh, it wasn't exactly like that—"

"Nonsense," my father cuts me off. "Your mother is right. We're here for you, and we have been from the day you were born." He winks, and it makes me smile. I forgot he used to wink at me when we were up to something. Usually, it came with promises of ice cream. I don't know how I even remember as much, but I do.

"Does this mean you have ice cream waiting for me too?"

His mouth drops, surprise overcoming him. He booms out a laugh and tugs me toward the refrigerator. "I can't believe you remember," he admits when my mom moves to sit at the table away from us.

"Of course. I never forgot you, either of you," I embellish, sending a glance in my mom's direction.

He hugs me to his side and opens the freezer. "Let's find the good stuff. I know the cook keeps our favorites."

"Mine too?" I ask, shocked to my core. I don't remember what it is, so I'll have to pretend I do.

My mom calls from the table, "Your father stopped eating his favorite. He always has a pint in the freezer, but he goes for yours instead."

I meet his gaze. It's watery, but I let it pass without acknowledgment. My parents love me, and they've never stopped. If I doubted as much before, I don't anymore. It's in all the little things I've noticed since coming here to my home. They never stopped believing I was out there somewhere, and it fills my heart full of love. Having them in my life now far outweighs the negativity coming from Diana. I can deal with her if it means I have my parents around to cushion her blows.

CHAPTER 13

HUNTER

"I overheard Steven's conversation this morning. My niece is searching for three friends she had on the island with her. We need to find them before she does. I don't want anyone else miraculously showing up and causing any more problems. The biker was enough," Diana gripes at her partner. I still haven't figured his name out. She doesn't seem to respect him to call him anything at all. She merely complains and barks orders his way every chance she gets.

"What do you know about them?"

"Only their names. Laura, Luna, and Mary. They sound familiar, but I can't place them. Were they the caretaker's daughters? I recall you saying Aura was with other little girls when you took her, but I was under the impression they were toddlers."

He shakes his head. "No, there were three girls playing and looking after Aura when I had the opportunity to snatch her, but they weren't toddlers. I took them all and sold them to the same man. They were old enough to recognize and point me out... I'd say about ten years old or so. I don't know enough about kids to say for sure."

"How on earth did you get them all to go with you? Kids are wretched little beasts, especially when they're young."

"Gave them some of the drugs I'd brought for Aura. They were too stupid to say no to free candy, especially since I work for the estate."

"You work for me," Diana clarifies.

"I care for you," he states in return.

She ignores him completely, turning on the large computer screen against the far wall. She begins searching through employee records until she finds a particular woman. She searches her name next, and sure enough, the images of three little girls pop up. They were eight, ten, and twelve when taken on the same occurrence as Aura.

How could I have not known they were the daughter of another employee here? Was I too young and headstrong to only focus on Aura and not anyone else? I suppose I was blinded by her beauty and significance to me to notice anything else when it all happened. I was immature and too inexperienced to know where to start in a kidnapping case. Her disappearance is what spurred me on to become a bounty hunter. Though, endless searches leading nowhere with her had me picking up cases in the areas I thought she may have ended up in. It turns out they were all dead ends, and she'd been off the grid for so long, no one would've recognized her if they saw her.

She randomly blurts out, "Can you believe my niece had the audacity to ask if I'd seen the biker?" She gestures in my direction. "Wanted to know if I'd spoken to him again before he'd left. She's so entitled it makes me sick."

I call out, "I told you! She's not the only one looking for me either, I guaran-damn-tee it. You're going to get caught, and the pain will be real unless you let me go and escape. You're running out of time, my brothers are coming for me, and they'll want blood."

Her lackey screams, "Shut up!" He rushes me, delivering a swift kick to my head.

I struggle to remain coherent.

As I'm fading out of consciousness, I hear Diana murmur, "Not long now, indeed. We haven't given him any water or anything, so he'll lose his fight soon enough. Before long, he'll become delirious and not know up from down."

AURA

Tears fill my eyes as I think about Hunter. Something's wrong. Not only do I feel it in my stomach, but my heart has been hurting since last night. When I told my mother, she insisted I see her physician, but the doctor only came back to say it was my intuition, and I should follow it. I don't know how the doctor knew what I needed to hear, but I'm grateful for her advice.

I glance at the guy sitting in the back of the car with me as I anxiously wait. My father finally took my requests seriously and got his driver to bring me to Hunter's place. The catch being is that I had to bring one of his security men along with me in case Hunter truly is in some sort of danger. The guy kind of gives me hostile vibes, but I'm chalking it up to not being around many men in my lifetime. I spent most of my years with three women, so it's strange, but I'm beginning to adjust. Being with Hunter was a good chance for me to see how men can be and not to fear them.

"We're here, Miss Aura," the driver announces.

I flash a grateful smile. "Thank you." My hand reaches for the door handle as I'm ready to leap out and run to the front door, but my arm's grabbed, securing me in place. My stare spins to the man sitting near me. "What do you think you're doing?" I demand.

He offers a stern frown. "My job is to keep you safe. Remain in the car until I've walked the perimeter and deemed it not a threat."

I snatch my arm away. "While I appreciate your concern, you work for my family, including me. I'll walk around the house with you."

He begins to argue, but I jump out of the car regardless. I meant what I said, I respect his job, but no one will give me orders and not expect a fight from me in return. "If Hunter notices you here alone, you won't receive a warm welcome," I mutter as I stride alongside the bodyguard. I doubt Hunter will be thrilled about me being alone with a man and bringing him here, but what does he expect when he doesn't answer anyone's phone calls?

I smell the rose bushes as my newfound partner does his search around the backside of the house. Glancing around, the first thing I notice is it doesn't look like he's been here. He'd usually waters his plants on the back porch and leaves trails of water all over the place. He eventually let me take over the chore, along with a few others. I try the door handle, finding it locked, but it normally would be. I knock on the back door rather than backtrack and circle to the front. Surely, he'd know it's a friend if I'm back here. I knock again, and a third time, before eventually I begin to beat on the door rattling the nearby windows.

"Miss," I'm interrupted. "He doesn't seem to be home. Maybe we should leave and try another time. He may be on a job or something."

"Or something. No, we won't be leaving. Can you, uh… break the door?"

He clears his throat, "I'm sorry, what? You'd like me to break the door in? You're asking me to willingly commit a crime?"

Well, it doesn't sound so smart when he puts it like that, but I nod anyway. "Yes, break it down. Oh, and just to warn you, there will be a loud noise. Don't be frightened, it will shut off," I reassure, then quietly murmur, "Somehow." Hopefully, Hunter will show up and turn the blasted alert thing off.

"I can't believe I'm doing this," the guy mutters, then steps back. He lifts his leg and gives the door a few good kicks. If I knew that's how you do it, then I'd have done it myself. The door swings open, crashing into the wall behind it, then flings back in our direction. Luckily, security guy, Ely, I believe he told me his name, grabs the door in time. The shrill alarm blares to life, making my hands fly over my ears. The sound gives me goosebumps and causes every hair on my arms to stand at attention.

"I can't stand the retched noise," I comment and step past him. He's not a fan and tugs me behind him as he glances around the room, gun drawn.

"Hunter!" I scream as loudly as possible, making Ely jump in surprise. "You're going to accidentally shoot yourself. Pay attention," I chastise, and he offers me a testy glare. Needless to say, this adventure hasn't gotten off to a good start, but I'm determined to find out something to put my mind at ease.

Ely clears the house with me hot on his heels, but Hunter's nowhere to be found. "Do you know where he keeps any contacts? You could call a sibling or friend to see if they've heard from him. I'm telling you this is all unnecessary, the guy probably wants some space."

Not my Hunter, I know him.

He likes his space here, away from others, not the other way around.

I don't say as much, but rather, "Where would a guy keep those things?"

"Usually, close to a laptop. Does he have a spot he uses or keeps his computer?"

I nod frantically and take off in a run toward the kitchen. I think I remember passing a note with a number on it. I nearly collide with the kitchen counter as I race into the kitchen and round the counter to the refrigerator. On the side right where I remember it is a sticky note with letters and numbers.

Briar landline 553-0119 is scribbled in Hunter's writing. I show it to Ely, not being able to read it. "Does this say anything we can use?" I ask.

He stares at me quizzically before he finally nods. "Yeah. It says Briar landline. You know who that is?"

"Oh, yes! It's a good friend of Hunter's."

"There you go then. The note you have is the number to his house phone."

I flash a grateful smile. "Perfect. Let's get out of here, the noise is giving me a headache."

"Thought you'd never ask," he mutters and props a chair under the back door handle to keep the door closed. I follow him out the front, where he manages to close the door and somehow keep it locked at the same time. The guy is good and seems to know what he's doing.

As soon as I'm back in the car and the alarm is mere background noise as we drive away, I pull my new phone free. I use it exactly how my father showed me, and before I know it, the phone is ringing.

"Who is this?" is answered with a deep growl.

"Hello to you too. Not a friendly way to answer your phone, just so you know."

"Who is this?" he repeats.

"It's Aura. I was hoping you could help me."

He sighs, not in a rude way, but more relieved. "Anything, anytime. What do you need?"

"I haven't heard from Hunter since he brought me home, and I'm worried. He's never stopped talking to me. I know I haven't been around long, but it's strange. I don't feel right inside when I think about him, and it's scaring me," I eventually admit, not wanting to hold my emotions inside any longer.

"Okay, have you tried calling his cell?"

"Yes, and he hasn't answered. Not for me, my parents, or his parents."

"Whoa, already calling in the calvary."

I don't know what he means, so I continue, "And I just broke into his house. He wasn't home."

"Clearly, if you had to break in. Hunter may be a recluse, but he'll still shoot if someone's on his property. You'd have known he was home the moment you pulled in the driveway."

"The alarm thing was set off again, so he may be upset about it."

He chuckles. "No worries. I'll call and take care of it. I'm on his approved list and have the code to make it shut off. Anything else you can tell me?"

"I've been calling for two days and nothing."

"Hmm. Let me call around to a few people and see if they know where our boy is at. If they don't have a lead, I'll try pinging his cell. Is this your number?"

"This phone is mine, but I don't know the number."

"I have it. It popped up on my TV when you first called."

"Okay, so now what do I do?"

"You hang tight, keep yourself safe, and I'll call you soon."

"Please hurry, my heart is hurting. I know something's not right."

"Funny, he said the same thing happened to him when he found you."

"Really?"

"You didn't hear me say it. I'm hanging up now. I'll call soon."

"Thanks, bye," I say, but he's already gone.

I glance at Ely to find him staring at me, eyebrows raised. "Any news?"

I shake my head. "No, but Briar will find him."

I hope.

If he can't, then I may lose my mind altogether at this rate.

I knew I should've never let him leave the party the way he did.

CHAPTER 14

AURA

Briar didn't get ahold of Hunter either. Thankfully, he called a bunch of his other friends to come and help us with our search. I told them everywhere we'd been in the past week and anything I could possibly remember about the day of the party. It's been three days since Hunter's been missing now, and I'm a complete mess. One part of me wants to curl up in a ball and sob with worry, while the other wants to search nonstop until I find him.

The problem is I have no idea where to go or what to do. Everyone tells me to relax and not to worry, but it seems to be the only thing I can do. I've been pacing, but it barely takes the edge off my errant thoughts. At this point, I've spoken to Hunter's parents more than my own. They're just as worried as I am, and it breaks me each time I hear their voices, and I have to tell them I have no new information. I've never felt so helpless in my entire life. Could this be a snippet of what my parents went through with my disappearance? This is horrible.

"We'll find him," my father attempts to reassure me for the millionth time, but it's no use. I want so badly to yell and scream with my frustration, to tell them they lost me for most of my life, so why should I believe them now? Hunter is everything to me, and I refuse to sit back and watch as he disappears through my fingers forever.

"I just can't believe no one saw him leave. The last place his cell gave a signal was here, and his vehicle is still here. It doesn't make sense. He couldn't get locked somewhere?"

"No, I've already told you, Aura. My staff has searched this place high and low."

I can't help but wonder if they've lied to him. This house is massive, and it'd be easy to overlook somewhere. I went wandering several times and ended up lost, needing someone to show me my way back. Hunter has been here several times, but I doubt he's gone to every room in the past, so it's possible he ended up lost as well. Still, someone should've discovered him by now. His friends have shown up, demanding to search the house, but my father's put his foot down. He swears the staff can handle it, but he's allowed them along with me to search the surrounding grounds, and there's no trace of Hunter anywhere. If I hadn't seen him with my own eyes that night, it'd be easy to believe he was never here in the first place.

I head to my room at a loss, full of disappointment. I feel so helpless, and I hate it. What good is having all this money if it can't help you find the people you care about? It seems to me being wealthy is more of a burden than a benefit. I continue my pacing in my room, tugging at my hair. It's crazy today, but I couldn't be bothered to twist it up or anything. My mind's been on one thing only, and it hasn't been my hair.

Briar sends a message into the group text, but I have no idea what it says. I mess with the phone a bit more, attempting to call him when it magically reads his message aloud. At least, I hope it's what the text says.

Briar: *Aura, we've found nothing. Have you? Our*

brother would've reached out to us by now. I'm beginning to think something foul is at play here. No more time to fuck around, we need to find him now.

I hit the button, and it lets me talk, transcribing my words. I don't know if it replies with the correct things I say or not, but I try.

Aura: *I've felt this way for days. Please find him.*

They don't respond, and I nearly call them but change my mind at the last minute. I think of the people we saw the night of my welcome-home party. There were so many faces, any of them could've seen Hunter, yet no one has come forward with information. My father said he went over Aunt Diana's evening in detail, however, her name keeps nagging me in the back of my head. Is it because of her icy welcome she's shown me, or could it be something else entirely? She's family, I shouldn't think of her this way, but I do.

What would it hurt if I asked her again? Maybe she'll remember something new. One thing's for certain, I can't see the evil queen looking a total mess. She wasn't fond of my jeans and leather the other day, so that's exactly what I'll be wearing. I need any advantage to throw her off-kilter a bit, and if I can achieve as much with an outfit, I'm definitely going to try my luck. Something tells me Diana is a worthy adversary, and I need to find out what makes her tick.

I hop in the shower, grateful for some semblance of a plan, no matter how small it may be.

HUNTER

A noise rouses me from the uncomfortable nap I was taking. Not by choice or anything but after being kicked in the fucking head, I've been dozing off randomly. I have a concussion, I can tell by the way certain things become blurry, and I feel nauseous from time to time. There's also my memory turning foggy occasionally and the falling asleep. Fuck, I hate this shit. I make a terrible captive. I won't plead or cave, so I basically just lay here and rot.

Diana's henchman took me for two bathroom breaks since I've been here and none today I'm aware of. I'm pretty sure I'm all out of fluids, and it will only further help to fuck me up. I need to be alert and strong, so the first shot of freedom I have, I can take it. Knowing what she said about me becoming dehydrated is starting to come true only serves to piss me off even more. With the anger comes a rush of clarity. There's something going on—yelling or arguing. I don't know if the voices belong to Diana and her goon, but I suppose they do. Good, I hope they rip each other's fucking eyeballs out and slowly bleed to death.

This situation damn sure didn't go how I anticipated. I've been beaten up fairly badly in the past by random criminals, so this shouldn't faze me, yet it does. Not due to my failure to escape, but because Aura's safety and well-being are on the line. I despise feeling helpless and fucking worthless. With a painful scowl, I try to glance around the room. It's not an easy feat since the past few times I've attempted as much, I've nearly puked my guts up. My hands fist, my fingers biting into my flesh to keep my vision clear.

"You haven't seen him? You're a hundred percent sure?" I hear in the background. "Why do I find your lack of information hard to believe?" The voice is familiar, yet it doesn't hit me yet.

I try to speak, but nothing leaves my lips. Shaking my head, I try again, "Hello?" My head rings with the words, and so help me, I wish I could grip it and rest it in my palms, but there's no way for it to happen since my hands are tied up. I try to wiggle my body, but it's too sore and stiff to do much of anything.

"I heard something."

More arguing. I feel like my mind's going to blow apart. I must only be catching bits and pieces of their conversation.

"No! You'll let me through right now because I said so. Move."

I blink, and then Aura's storming into the room. My eyes widen, shocked to see her, but also not sure if she's real. "Hunter!" she screams when she notices me. Diana comes up behind her, and I remember why I want Aura anywhere but here.

"Behind you," I manage to groan and watch Aura spin around. She's just in time to dodge Diana's swing with a big black vase. I'd put money the monstrosity is made of thick glass and would knock my woman out.

"My knife's on her desk." I attempt to concentrate on what needs to be done, rather than lead by my emotions. We have a minuscule window before Diana comes up with a way to hurt Aura or call for backup, and I need to be free before then.

Aura tosses a desk chair and manages to clip Diana's side with it.

"Bitch!" Diana growls. "This time I'll make sure you're dead!" she threatens.

Aura pays her no mind, grabbing my long knife. She quickly unsnaps the handle and pulls it free from the case. "Stay away from me," she demands, holding the blade securely. She points it toward her aunt, looking ready to jab if necessary. My woman is fierce, not looking the slightest bit intimidated to be facing off with her abductor.

"I told you it was only a matter of time." I mock in Diana's direction, distracting her. The moment she turns her head my way to yell at me, Aura shoots off in my direction. She doesn't stop until she's behind me with the blade.

"Stay back, I swear to God, I'll stab you with this thing," Aura warns, sounding beyond pissed off. She's ready to fly off the handle like a rabid dog to protect me, and I'm so damn proud.

"You'll do no such thing, you're harmless. Besides, I have just what I need to put you to sleep for good."

"Place the blade in my hands, my love, and prepare to defend yourself," I coax, hoping like hell Aura remembers the few moves I taught her during her stay with me. I need her to go full-on girl fight with her aunt while I work to get myself free.

She does as I ask, leaning down to place the blade in my hands. They're numb, so I use every bit of concentration and strength to hold it. I could drop it, and I'd probably never feel it, but thankfully, it doesn't happen. Aura leaps over my body, getting in the defensive position I taught her. While they yell back and forth, threatening each other, I work at sawing the rope around my body. My blade is sharp as fuck, so the line across my back snaps fairly quickly. I'm able to sit up on my knees and point the knife down to cut the rope securing my feet.

A loud crash echoes, snapping my attention back to the women. Aura's throwing anything she can find at her aunt while Diana scrambles to touch Aura with the plant she brought down here, swearing it will kill Aura. It's all the extra motivation I need, quickly rolling my legs in front of me and using my feet to hold my knife still enough to saw my hands free.

The rope snaps just as Diana's accomplice rushes into the room. I snatch my truth seeker up and run for him. He was never expecting me to be free and come at him. He also didn't realize I had my favorite weapon in hand. He roars as his fingers reach for my throat, and my blade sinks deep into his belly. He gapes, stunned to his core. His mouth moves, opening and closing several times before I twist the handle and drive it to his side. It's long and sharp enough that it'll pierce his kidneys, and he'll painfully bleed out. He deserves it, they both do after everything they've done. Speaking of, I twist around, allowing his dead weight to drop.

Diana lunges for Aura again, this time tossing the plant at my woman. The leaves gaze her flesh, and I see red. Charging for Diana, I waste no time with a hefty slice to her throat. Blood splatters everywhere, and in a fit of rage, I stab her straight through the heart. "Fuck you dead, bitch. I told you to stay away from my woman."

"Hunter," my name's whispered, then repeated. Aura keeps saying it, each time a little louder than the one before. "Look at me, Hunter, I'm okay, and we're safe. You killed them both, they can't hurt us. Please look at me and tell me you're all right. You've got dried blood all over you. Please, I want to touch you."

Eventually, I manage to shake myself out of my foggy haze. The adrenaline saved us. If it weren't for the natural burst of energy and clarity my body provided, I never would've been able to fight them off Aura. She would've died down here alongside me.

Fuck. *She got hit with the plant!*

I leap to my feet and charge in her direction.

Her hands go up in surrender. "It's only me! P-please, Hunter, you're scaring me!"

Stalling in my steps, I glance over myself as much as possible without a mirror. I was heading her way with my knife in her direction, completely covered in blood. Not to mention my injuries, I probably look like a fucking monster coming for her. Dropping the blade to the floor, I meet her stare and offer her my palm, facing upward.

It's all the reassurance she needs before she leaps for me, our bodies colliding. She wraps her arms around me tightly, tears pouring over her cheeks as she presses kisses to my cheeks. "I was so-so worried. I've been going crazy for days. I knew something wasn't right. I promise I've been searching for you."

"Well, you found me," I offer a grin and press a kiss to her forehead.

Everything dims and goes black as I hear her shouting my name, but it's okay.

She's safe.

CHAPTER 15

AURA

"Tell me he's all right," I bombard my father as soon as the doctor speaks to him. He was the only one he'd talk to, so the rest of us are left in the dark until he shares the news.

He holds his hand up and nods. "Try to calm down. I know you're worried, but it won't help to be worked up."

"Calm down? The man I love was held captive for who knows how long, then passed out in my arms. He means everything to me. Don't tell me to be calm."

My mom pulls me into a hug. "You heard her, sweetie. She has every right to be upset."

"You love him?" he asks, tilting his head with raised brows.

I give him a jerky nod, biting down on my cheek to stop myself from demanding he put me out of my misery where Hunter is concerned. I'm ready to storm into his hospital room and see him for myself. The 'only family' rule is bullshit, and the moment his parents arrive, I'm going into the room with them.

"He's suffered a concussion. There have been multiple hits to the back of his head. Diana and her helper weren't kind to him. I'm sorry." My mother and I both gasp. He continues, "The doctor and nurses have cleaned the cuts and stitched him up. Shaved his head, so that will be interesting."

I say a silent prayer for all his glorious hair. It'll grow back, but I'm not sure how Hunter will feel about it missing.

"He has rope burn in several spots, a dislocated shoulder, which they reset, and was dehydrated. He had a rough run, but he still managed to hold his own when it mattered most."

Tears cascade over my cheeks as the reality of how injured he is hits me full force. This is my fault. If he weren't always looking out for me, he'd be fine right now. "I can't believe this happened," I say after a beat.

My dad takes me from my mom's grip, wrapping his arms around me and tucking my body into his chest. The tears come like a waterfall, and I cry hard. I need it and don't give a second thought to who else is in the hospital with us as the tears fall from my face. To think this entire nightmare is finally over is an overwhelming relief but also hard to believe. "He's hurt, and it's my fault," I mutter into my father's shirt.

A strong squeeze on my shoulder has me lifting my head. I meet the pensive stare of a massive guy. He looks utterly miserable, frowning severely. I flick my gaze to Briar and a few other guys.

The big mean-looking dude says, "It's not your fault, honey. Hunter wouldn't have put himself in the position to protect you if he didn't want to be there. Trust me, he'd be much worse off if it were you in that room and him out here."

Briar squeezes my shoulder next, offering me a tender smile. "He's right. These are our brothers. We were all there when Hunter found you. They're in our group chat we've been texting in. They were following other leads when I came to help search your family's property, or they would've been there as well."

I offer them a shaky, grateful smile.

"Diablo," Briar continues and gestures to the frowner, then "Charmer," he says, and the handsome guy offers me a wide smile full of perfect pearly white teeth. "Last but not least, Malevolent." The man with a tall black mohawk nods his greeting. "I'm sure you'll meet Beast soon, as well as a few guys from his charter. He's further out of town, so it'll take him a while to stop in. Probably show up in the middle of the night and may have a woman with him. If he does, don't freak out. He doesn't care to deal with people if he can help it."

I sniffle and nod. "I won't, promise. Nice to meet all of you. I'm glad Hunter has friends." They chuckle at my words and take their seats, leaving me to my thoughts again.

"I'm glad he has a lot of support. Philip's always been a good kid."

"Call him Hunter, Dad."

His face lights up at me calling him Dad. "If he wants me to stop calling him by his name, then I will."

"When can I see him?"

"Soon," he replies as two people come rushing in our direction.

They're Hunter's parents, I'd know them anywhere. He looks so much like his father, and he had the same color hair as his mom before they shaved it all off. The couple eagerly greets my parents with hugs, and at some point, I'm pulled in as well. There are lots of tears from all of us, and then they go into Hunter's room to visit.

I'm trying to be patient, but it's hard. The last time I saw him, he was falling over, unconscious and covered in blood. I was terrified he was dead as well and never screamed so loudly in my life. A few of the staff heard the noise and came to check it out, then they alerted my father. He found me completely hysterical and had a private helicopter take Hunter and us to the hospital. Everyone followed us here, including the police. I haven't spoken to them yet, but I've already been warned I'll have to.

"My dear, you're so flushed. What's all over you?" my mother asks. "Is that a rash?"

"Oh no," I mutter and shake my head.

"What is it?" my parents ask at the same time, worry lacing

their tones.

"Diana had a plant. She threw it at me, and Hunter was trying to warn me," I share and begin itching all over the place. "Why am I so itchy? I was fine. I don't understand."

Without skipping a beat, my mom runs for the nurse counter, yelling she needs help.

This day is never going to end, I swear.

Ending up getting my own bed to rest in, the nurse gives me a shot for my allergic reaction. This time around, I'll be getting a prescription for extra EpiPens in case this happens again, and I'm not at a hospital. It's not the highlight of my trip, but I'll take a thousand needles if it means I can have Hunter safe and well with me again.

I haven't stopped daydreaming of him from the moment I met him, and it's only gotten stronger with time. Hard to imagine we've only been together intimately once when it feels like there's so much more between us sexually. Perhaps it's the lack of intimacy this past week, making me feel more connected to him than ever. You'd think it would be the opposite but being apart has only made me hold on to him harder, internally. My heart and mind have both decided it's Hunter they want, and there's no turning back now. I even admitted I'm in love with him to my father. He took it better than I expected, but he's already fond of Hunter, so I suppose I shouldn't have been surprised.

"Can I see him now?" I ask my mother as she enters the room with nurse Michelle. She's been great and in here several times to check on me.

Michelle offers me a warm smile. "Soon, let me check over your rash, and if it's gone down some more, then we'll sneak you into Mr. Philip's room. I still recommend running a full panel test of allergen and sensitivities. If you have this type of reaction to one plant, then there's bound to be another out there somewhere. Better to be prepared somewhat."

My mother nods. "Yes, I completely agree. What do you think, my dear?"

"Yes, it's a good idea. I don't want to go through this again or worry anyone when it might be able to be prevented."

They both smile in response, and Michelle goes about checking me over. "It's improving, which is exactly what we want. I see no reason why you can't visit your boyfriend. I know you're worried about him, but he's already looking better and will be back to himself soon."

I grin. "He's a biker with a heart of gold. Hopefully, his shoulder doesn't bother him too much. He likes to ride his motorcycle everywhere."

"He's a strong guy, so I'm sure he'll manage."

I hop out of bed, reaching for my shoes in a rush. She doesn't have to tell me twice, and I'm ready to run down the hall. I hadn't thought to ask before now if he's still passed out. I don't want to wake him up when I know he needs the rest. "Should I be quiet, or..." I trail off.

"He's coherent, but last I checked, he was sleeping. His body has been through a lot the past few days and needs rest to recuperate. The best thing to do is wait for him to rouse himself and speak quietly. His head will most likely hurt for a while from the concussion and stitches."

"Okay. Thank you for all of your help."

"It's what I'm here for. I love helping others... be well."

I hurry from the room, feet not moving fast enough, in my opinion, but I can't run in here so this is the best I can do. Diablo sits in the corner of his room, silent and stoic. Everyone has had a chance to come in and check on Hunter except me. I'm not bitter about it. Okay, so maybe just a touch salty, but I'm glad he has people here for him.

"Diablo," I whisper in greeting.

He tips his head. "I'll let you get your time in."

"I don't want to interrupt."

"I've been here a while, so it's fine. None of us want him to be alone."

Hunter groans. "Quit fussing over me, Mother Hen, and go find something to do."

Diablo chuckles and flips him off even though Hunter's eyes remain shut. "Take care of him. If he gives you any shit, a swift kick will shut his ass up," Diablo offers, wearing a smirk as he leaves.

I rush to the bedside, taking one of Hunter's hands in mine. "I'm so sorry this happened." I stare worriedly in the dim room.

He parts his lids, licks his lips, and says, "You have nothing to be sorry for. I never should've left you."

I shake my head. "No, it wasn't your responsibility to hold my hand through everything. You've already done way more than ever expected."

"I'd do it again if you needed me to."

"Why do I know you're not lying? You've got a good soul, Hunter. Thank you for helping me so much."

"My heart wants you, Aura, so I'd do anything for you." He tugs on my grip, pulling me from my seat.

"Be careful, I don't want you to hurt yourself."

"I'm fine, just have a little knot on my head somewhere."

I snort but lean in closer. There's so much more going on than a bump to the head, but I don't need to say it aloud. He knows it as well as I do but, of course, he doesn't care. Stubborn brute.

"I want you next to me. Climb in so I can hold you."

My eyes begin to tear up, feeling sappy to my soul over this handsome guy. He's been through hell, and yet he still wants to hold me. "I don't want to hurt…" I repeat, and he yanks me forward. I careen over him, my body sprawling on his. I try to jump back with a gasp, but he won't budge.

"Get in bed, woman," he orders, and this time around, I listen, not willing to deny him. I snuggle up to his side as he wraps his arm around me, securing me to him. My hand falls to his chest as I gaze up at him in wonder. Even in a hospital bed and injured, he feels so strong and solid. How do men do that?

"I missed you," I quietly admit and press a gentle kiss to his chin. His face is bruised up a bit, but not too badly. I have a feeling if he were to peel this hospital gown off, his body would tell a different story. I'm not ready to hear it, although something tells me it'll have a happy ending.

CHAPTER 16

HUNTER

Aura is still tucked into my side, warm and secure, when I wake up again. It's much more peaceful having her around—my body's at ease when she's in my arms. Glancing at the window blinds, the area has a light glow to it, letting me know it's dawn. It means we still have a bit of time before the hustle and bustle begins around here, and we're disturbed from our small cocoon of privacy. I could imagine waking up to her like this every day, minus the injuries and hospital bed.

I stare at Aura, taking in each detail I can make out in the dim lighting, cataloging them to memory. If she attempts to move on in her life without me, I don't know if I'll be able to handle it. We've been through too much in our short time together, we're bonded forever, and my heart's all in. Leaning closer, I press a kiss to the tip of her nose, then each cheek, her chin, and finally her lips.

She answers by leaning into the kiss and moving her hand up my chest to cradle my jaw. "Mmm," she groans, shifting a bit before pulling away to tiredly open her gorgeous eyes and gaze at me. "How are you feeling?" she asks, when it should be me concerned over how she's doing after everything we went through yesterday. I've probably traumatized her in some aspect with all the brutality she saw radiate from my ass in my fit of losing control. It's not as if I could help it, though, they'd threatened her, and I had to do what I could to protect her. I always will, and I'll never apologize for caring for her.

"Better. I can focus, and my head's no longer pounding."

"Good, and everywhere else?"

I shrug and smirk. "I've been hit before. Won't be the first or the last, beautiful. I think having you beside me helped the most, though. You kept me company all night."

She offers me a sleepy smile, reminding me of my nickname for her. She'll always be my sweet snoozing beauty with rosy cheeks and a shy smile.

"I was so scared when I couldn't find you," she confesses as her brows wrinkle with worry.

I don't care for it one bit. I want her happy. Everything's over and in the past, so she doesn't need to think about any of it. "You found me and saved my life by showing up when you did. Guess we're even now, huh? I should start calling you super beauty instead of snoozing beauty, I suppose."

My teasing brings a smile to her lips, and my chest feels like it may explode from the way she makes me feel all gooey over her.

"Nope. You saved me from Diana, so I still owe you."

"Is this going to become a thing?" I ask, wearing a grin and moving my finger between us.

"Definitely." She laughs, rubbing her hand down my chest. Her touch has my mind focusing on one thing alone, and my cock decides it's a decent time to make his presence known. "Oh, hello there," she mutters, making me chuckle louder. She has this way about her, and it brings out a lighter side of me.

Reaching over, I caress her arm and then her side. I explore over her hip until I dip between the juncture of her thighs. Her eyes glaze over as she exhales. She stares longingly at me while I touch her intimately over her clothes. There's nothing I want more at the moment, and I've already had her once, so I go for it again. My fingers make quick work of flicking the button free and moving her zipper down on her jeans. I want her here and now, hospital be damned. I don't care who knows we're fucking as long as I can feel her heat wrapped around me.

My hand dips inside, under her delicate lace panties until I can feel her pussy lips. My fingertips graze over them, brushing her clit until she hums with need. Continuing my path, I explore lower, discovering her wetness. Dipping a digit inside her entrance, she moans, legs opening wider to take my touch. "Feel good?" I love hearing her words when I have her turned on. It's beyond sexy.

She nods, cheeks flushing the delicious shade of pink I crave to see on her. She eventually asks, "Can I touch you?"

"You never have to ask. I want your hands on me any way possible."

She licks her lips and moves her hand under the sheet and thin cover. I nearly groan from her eagerness alone. She's utterly remarkable, tilting me on my side with a mere stroke.

"Push the blanket down and pull this thing up so I can watch you." I gesture to the paper-thin gown they have me trussed up in. She does as I ask until my cock's proudly on display, her fist wrapped around the length. She pumps up and down until I'm feeling more and more dizzy, but for a completely new reason than my concussion. "Take your pants off, Aura, and climb onto my lap."

Her mouth pops open, and she stops moving. "What? No, I'll hurt you."

"Do you trust me?"

"Of course. Always."

"Then take your clothes off and get over here."

She thinks on it for a beat while my fingers press deeper. Her wetness coats my digits, soaking them with each pass, making me horny as fuck. Finally, after what feels like forever, she stops my hand and stands. She takes her shirt off first, and my eyes are glued to her. She's crazy sexy and has no clue. It only makes her even more attractive, in my opinion. Her pants leave her next, then the teasing pair of tiny panties I'd felt moments ago. She's braless, she always is, and it's still alluring as fuck when I catch a glimpse each time.

I reach for her, grabbing ahold of her hand to offer her some balance as she gets back on the bed, one knee at a time. Much more carefully than necessary, she lifts one leg over my muscular thighs, then perches her butt above me. She's hovering her dripping cunt just out of reach from where I want her most.

"Woman," I growl, desire lacing my voice. I'm trying like hell to hold back and be cautious, but I'm two seconds away from flipping her underneath me and thrusting deep. "I need to feel you. Slide on my cock and put me out of my misery, yeah?"

"It won't hurt?" She checks again.

I grin at her concern. She's so damn cute. "Nah, the only thing I can feel right now is you. Now put that perfect wet pussy on my cock so we can both feel better."

With a nod, she scoots forward until the head of my cock caresses her folds, dipping inside. We both quietly moan in unison. It's a tease, and yet I crave more. My hands go to her hips, holding them tightly so I can shift her over me, repeating the same move she made moments before. I want it again. She whimpers when my tip presses against her clit, and I'm done for. No more messing around, I want inside her immediately. I need to be buried to the hilt, her surrounding me everywhere.

"Ready?" I check, letting her know I'm handing the reins over. "You're in control here, so lower yourself as slowly as you need to." Or as quickly as you want to. Lord knows I won't mind. I'll probably shoot my load far too fast, but we could always go a second round where she'll get hers more than once.

She doesn't hesitate and slides quickly down my hard, thick cock. "Oh yes!"

"Fuck!" I pant, stunned she went the quick route and impaled her pussy on my cock right off the bat. Beads of sweat dot my brow as I attempt to breathe through the intense feelings. I didn't think it was possible for things to get any better between us but feeling her pussy raw and wet has me ready to beg for more. I'm clean, and I know she's only been with me, so I'm not worried about wrapping it up. This means too much between us, the undeniable intimacy and chemistry linking us together. I've fallen for her, and there isn't a doubt in my mind she's the one for me.

"What is it?" she pauses. "Are you okay?" she asks again, and I can no longer deal with being handled with kid gloves. I sit up, holding her to me to suck on her breasts, peppering random nips in between each taste. "Yes!" she calls as I bounce her hips, letting her know she can move and be as wild as she wants. I'll happily take whatever she wants to give me. She shifts forward then back, and I release my lips to hiss in relief.

"Christ, you feel phenomenal. You have the warmest, wettest, fluffiest pussy I've ever felt before, and it's life-changing." My body quakes as a twinge of pleasure shocks my body. My orgasm is way too close to the surface, and I have to concentrate hard to fight it back down. I want her to enjoy this, not have me coming in a record amount of time.

The door opens, with a nurse sticking her head in. "Oops!" She gapes for a beat then whispers, "I'll be back in ten minutes, please be careful. No sudden movements." She points to make her point, then she's gone just as quickly as she showed up.

I can't help myself, I burst out laughing as soon as the door closes, jostling Aura all over my lap. "I wasn't expecting anyone or her understanding," I admit, juggling Aura with each laugh. She grins, leaning in to kiss me. She keeps it much tamer than I want right now, but I go with it and let her lead the way as I offered before. I've missed her as well—her touch, taste, and everything else, not just her warm, wet cunt. "Mmm, slide down and rotate your hips."

"Bossy." She does as I instructed, causing us both to groan with pleasure. "No sudden movements, mister," she teases.

I can't help but grin against her mouth and kiss her again. "I don't plan on letting you out of my sight for a while," I admit. "I hope you're ready. I'm going to be inside you morning, noon, and night. Then I'm going to want to spend my meals with you and evenings doing nothing and everything."

"Good. I was hoping you'd feel that way because I do too. I've discovered I don't like being away from you, not even for a short amount of time. You make me comfortable and happy. I feel safe with you."

"As long as you want me, I'm yours. You have my word," I swear, aware of what the promise entails. I'm hers, and I certainly hope she's mine. "No other guys, just me and you," I declare because there's no way in hell I'm sharing her. I'd end up killing someone again if it went down that road.

She nods, shifting her hips left to right and back again. "Only us," she agrees, running her tongue from my throat to my shoulder. She pauses on the ball of my shoulder to bite, and her teeth in my flesh give me the best case of chills. Her hands caress me everywhere, and the sensations running through my body are consuming but in the best sort of way.

"You drive me crazy inside. I want you."

"You have me," she whispers, lifting, then falling on my cock swiftly. My eyes bulge with an impending orgasm coming at me again. I just fought the bastard off, and now it's knocking on my door again, ready to take the finish line. There's no way I'm letting loose without her popping off first. So my fingers find her clit, lightly applying pressure until she bows forward with a cry.

"You're not playing fair."

"Mmm. Can't wait to take you home, flip you on your back, and fuck you senseless. I probably won't make it to the bed, just shove you against the nearest wall or counter and make this sweet-as-sin pussy come all over me. Maybe bend you over the couch so every time you sit on it, you'll remember me making you come in the same spot."

"Oh God!" She moans loudly as her walls clamp around my cock, squeezing me firmly enough I see double. Not concussion-related, thank fuck.

Her pussy pulses, and my cock throbs in response.

"You like it a little dirty, don't you?"

She nods, rocking forward then back, sweat droplets rolling down the valley of her breasts. They're so damn enticing, I can't hold back from sucking one into my mouth. I let it pop out after I play awhile and pluck at her tender clit until her body's shaking in my hold.

"Look at me," I demand. "Come all over my dick. I want this pussy gushing all over me until I'm coming so hard my fucking toes curl."

My free hand moves to her silky locks, fist curling in the long length. I give it a generous tug as I pop my hips upward at the same time. I manage to do it twice more before she's crying out with her intense release. She fucking floods me, and I follow up with my own orgasm. I wasn't kidding about how good she feels, my toes curl, and my eyes roll heavenward. I come so hard I feel like I've just lost five pounds.

"Damn," I pant, falling backward and making my head scream with irritation. I ignore it because I have someone far more important to concentrate on. "I swear it was better than last time, but it was amazing before... so it's hard to accurately judge."

"What would help?"

"We need to keep doing it," I reply deadpan, and she giggles. I fucking love the sound more than anything else in the world, and I swear I want to hear it from her several times every day.

She ducks into the bathroom, freshening up, and returns with a wet washcloth. "I can shower, babe, it's all good." I've never had a woman clean me up before, and I'm not too sure how I feel about it. I should be the one getting the cloth for her, taking care of her needs, not the other way around.

She tilts her head to the side and pushes her bottom lip out into a pout. Right then and there, I know I'm utterly fucked if she catches on to what the look does to me. "Please let me take care of you, Hunter. I want to do it."

I clear my throat and offer her a quick nod. If it'll make her happy, I'm for damn sure not turning down the extra attention from her. Hell, if she keeps the pout up, I don't have a fighting chance when it comes to anything. She swiftly pulls her shirt on and perches on the side of the small, uncomfortable bed. Carefully, she wipes my thighs and abdomen before moving to my cock. She rinses the towel clean and comes back to continue her sweet torture. Each rotation of her hand only serves to turn me on all over again. I'm like a spring chicken where fucking her is concerned, and I don't think I'll ever have my fill of this amazing woman next to me.

"Your bruises look painful. Can I do anything to make them feel better?"

With my mind in the gutter, I grin, and she swats at me with a laugh.

"You asked." I shrug and adjust to get as comfortable as I can. The bed is small for a guy my size, the mattress too thin and the sheets scratchy. I shouldn't complain, I'm here for medical treatment, not a vacation. But still, healing would be a bit better if it weren't so bare-bones in here. I can probably talk my parents into donating. It's the least my family can do after all the drama of having us here.

"We need to get you out of here, so we're not interrupted again," Aura adds, which I'm a hundred percent ready for. She wants me to get better for fucking purposes, and I'm completely down for it. She should probably be careful what she wishes for in that sense.

"Okay. I'll concentrate on showing the nurses I'm all right, but I'm sure the one who walked in would say I'm pretty much recovered. Some pussy therapy hit the spot."

"Oh my God." She rolls her eyes. "I'll see if I can find your doctor and get an estimate on when you can go home."

"I'm going home today, up to them if it's with their consent or not. Either way, I'm checking out of this spot and sleeping in my bed tonight."

She shakes her head. "Why am I just now learning you're not only bossy but also stubborn?"

"Hey, you're the one who seduced me earlier. I'm simply following through."

She snorts and shakes her head. "I recall you putting your hands on me first. I can't help it if I turn to putty when you touch me." She leans in and brushes a kiss across my lips.

I watch her leave the room, her words still ringing in my ears. She's not the only one who turns to mush. The woman already owns me and doesn't have the faintest clue. If she only realized she's always been mine, and we were destined from the moment I laid eyes on her.

CHAPTER 17

AURA

"We've found them," Hunter greets as soon as I come inside, closing the back door behind me. I was checking on the expansive garden he's helped me build and plant. It's all new and fresh, needing plenty of love and attention. When I asked him if it was all right to add more garden back there, I don't think he was anticipating what I had in mind. I've always loved nature, and not living in it as I was before has made me a touch stir-crazy. My parents were thrilled to discover I have the family green thumb, and they let me have my pick of what I wanted from their farms and green/grow houses. To say I've gone a bit overboard is an understatement, and I'm sure the creatures will thank me for the new variety of food they'll pop over to eat for a late-night snack.

I offer the handsome man a warm smile and follow it up with a slow, tender kiss. Time has only gotten better with Hunter. I didn't think it was possible to be any happier than when I initially got home, but he's proved me wrong. I was head over heels for him fairly quickly, and now I'm hopelessly in love with him. It was a shock to learn Hunter has killed people in the past, but after witnessing the situation with Diana and her accomplice, there was no holding it back. Who am I to judge him? He saved me, took care of me, and makes me smile every day, so he's a good man in my opinion. He says mine is the only one that counts anyhow.

"Who, my love?" I ask, heading for his beloved coffee maker to make us a cup. We share most things—foods, drinks, showers, our time. If it can be done together, then we're doing it. The only time he strays away from me is if I'm spending time alone with my parents or he has a job. I usually use his work as time to spend with my family, though, so we hit two birds with one stone. I keep trying to talk him into letting me come with him on a job, but he never budges. It's dangerous, and he wants me safe, so I respect his reasons.

I pour a steaming cup of the strong, dark liquid, add in a dash of Almond Joy creamer and two small spoonfuls of sugar. He doesn't like it too sweet, but I don't like it plain ether, so we compromise and meet in the middle. I blow on the steam and set the cup beside us as he responds.

"Your friends... Laura, Luna, and Mary."

I nearly fall over as I wasn't ever expecting to hear him utter those words. "Oh my God," I whisper. "Seriously? Wait... are they alive?" Heart pounding in my chest, anxiety for their wellbeing hits me full force. I've thought of them every single day since I've been here. This has become my home, and I've wanted more than anything to show them. I know they would be both proud and thrilled for me. I've wanted to go back to the island several times to try to find them, but my family begged me not to. I hated to give in and agreed not to go, but it's killed me not knowing how my friends were doing.

Hunter pulls me in, wrapping his strong grip around me. He makes me feel loved and cherished, especially when he holds me like this. He nods. "Yes. Not only are they alive, but they've come back home. They were so happy when the team found them. Well, they were terrified at first. Once they were reassured you were safe with pictures and their mother's been waiting, they jumped at the chance to return.

"They made it home?" I ask, wanting him to repeat his words. Tears crest as happiness consumes my soul. Everything feels right in the world now, finally. My friends are home and safe, Hunter loves me and is with me, I have my parents and a home, and lastly, Diana has paid for her crimes with her life.

He nods, and I tuck my face into his chest, squeezing him tightly as I'm overcome with emotions. "You really are a knight in shining armor, my prince."

He laughs but catches the seriousness in my tone. Pulling me back enough to meet my watery gaze, he says, "Only if you'll be my queen someday?"

I nod, lips trembling. Of course, I'll be his. I already am in my heart and soul. "Yes. I'd love to marry you."

He squeezes me tightly, pressing a loving kiss to my lips before asking, "You want to go see them?"

"Of course! Let me slip on some shoes, and then I'll be ready," I say and follow it up with a yawn.

"My beautiful woman, you're always so sleepy if you don't catch a quick nap. We can wait an hour or two."

"There's no way I'm wasting time sleeping when I could be visiting with more people I love. I'm too excited to sleep anyhow, so let's go."

He holds his hands up in surrender. "You got it, but you should probably switch shorts. You're covered in dirt."

I glance down, laughing. I hadn't noticed, and he's right, I'm a total mess from the garden. "Okay, so five minutes, tops, and we're out the door."

"Waiting on you," he calls as I take off in a jog to our room—another thing we share since he hasn't left my side from the moment he checked himself out of the hospital. I wanted him to move into my parents' house, but he wasn't having it. I can't blame him. I enjoy our privacy and love our home out here in the mountains. We still have my room at the mansion, so if there's a party or something else where we don't want to drive home, we can sleep over. I think the house creeps Hunter out after what happened, though, and I understand completely. I refuse to go back to the lower level. I wish my parents could destroy it without messing up their house, but it's not an option. I asked my father, and he looked into it. I think they're going to convert it into a bunker or storage sort of place where you'll need a special code to get in, so no one can hide someone down there ever again without one of us knowing.

I'm ready in record time. I've tossed on a pair of clean jean shorts, my leather jacket, favorite cowboy boots and have my hair thrown up into a messy bun. I grab my sunglasses on our way out, and we head for his bike, hand in hand.

Another first for both of us—a woman on the back of his bike and me riding. I love it. It makes me feel free, gliding along the open road with the wind in my wild hair. I begged him for a while, and once he finally gave in, our rides became a usual thing. Sometimes we'll meet up with his club brothers and ride together. He's even taken me to a few other clubhouses to visit with various presidents and their women. It's an interesting lifestyle, but overall, I'm glad Hunter has chosen to remain a Nomad. I like having him mostly to myself with the occasional visitor.

I climb on his big, shiny white beast, sliding behind my man, and wrap my hands around his trim waist. I never knew riding a motorcycle could be sexual, but with Hunter, it's hot, and we've had plenty of sexy times. Usually, we'll get so pent up for each other, he'll pull off on the side of a random road so we can have a bit of naughty fun before making it the rest of the way. Other times, he'll make me wait, and after holding him closely for a time, along with mixing in the adrenaline from the ride, it's a natural aphrodisiac for me. I basically end up attacking him the moment we're in the door.

His bike thunders down the windy road, the sound echoing in

the endless array of trees. It's peaceful out here away from everyone else, and after living on the island for most of my life, it's exactly what I need. I wasn't meant to be in a lavish mansion, living the life of a socialite. I could always have it if I change my mind, but I won't. Hunter and nature are all I need to be fulfilled in life.

In no time, it seems, we're pulling up in front of a small house. I don't remember it, so I don't think I ever came here when I was little. I know now I was on my parents' property playing with the three girls when we were all taken. I never knew much growing up, thinking our island life was normal in a sense after a while. I knew I had a family out in the world somewhere, and we all talked about missing them, but in a way, they never seemed real. I was a toddler, so I'm sure it was confusing for me, but children are resilient, and the four of us proved as much. It's a miracle we survived at all, and if the three girls hadn't been forced to grow up so quickly before their adoptions, we probably wouldn't have made it as long as we did.

Hunter turns his bike off and holds it steady, offering me his bicep to carefully climb off. I made the mistake in the past of rushing and burned myself. He practically had a cow and freaked on me being hurt, so now I take my time. He's also begun to teach me the basics of how to drive the motorcycle. In my opinion, it's far too heavy and imposing for someone like me, but we've discussed getting me a dirt bike or something similar to learn on. He toes the kickstand down and swings his leg over, coming to stand beside me. I grab for his hand, needing his silent strength he always seems to have an abundance of.

The front door opens with Luna rushing outside. We screech in excitement as soon as we see each other and race into the other's arms. We grip each other so tightly, I feel like one of us may burst, but I don't care. I finally have Luna in my arms, and I love her.

Mary and Laura are right behind, and soon we're all crying and pulling each other in for hugs. "I thought I'd never see you again,"

I confess to each of them as tears roll down my face. "This is my guy, Hunter. He's been searching for you from the moment I could remember your names."

"What do you mean, remember?" Mary asks, still holding my hand. "Did something happen to you?"

I nod. "I'm still not sure what exactly, but it caused me to lose some of my memories. They still haven't returned and may never."

Hunter cuts in, "We've been hoping you can fill in some pieces for us."

Laura replies, "Yeah, sure. I can try to help. I was with Aura the day we lost her."

My gaze snaps to hers as I attempt to put missing pieces together. What were we doing?

An older lady comes outside last and goes straight for Hunter. She wraps her arms around him and cries, thanking him repeatedly. "If it weren't for you searching and sending those people, I'd never have gotten my girls back. I can never thank you enough. The child protective office harassed me for years, believing I had something to do with their disappearance. Just because they each came from a different broken home and I adopted them, it doesn't mean I'd value their lives any less than my own. I was heartbroken. So devastated because I'd loved them so much already in the short time I had them. Please come inside and make yourself at home."

She finally lets him go, and we follow her into the house. Mary pulls me down on a couch next to her while Hunter takes my other side. Laura, Luna, and their mother take the adjacent couch. "You all look good, but it's weird seeing you in pants," I admit, causing them to laugh. They had weaved clothing, but it was always dresses since they were the least difficult. My own was the cloth of my old dress mixed with vines to cover me fully.

"What happened?" Hunter asks, cutting straight to the chase. I'm glad he's focused because my emotions are all over the place right now, and I can't think.

Laura speaks up. "We were collecting fallen coconuts when I saw someone." She meets my confused stare, saying, "You didn't see him. I didn't want to frighten you, so I never said anything about them. I told you to run back to the hut and remain there since we were out further than we usually went. Food was scarcer than usual that year, so we were forced to scout areas we wouldn't normally visit."

My stomach pangs, remembering us being hungry so often and not having any food. We never completely starved, but there were many rough times. I'm so grateful we never have to worry about going without food again.

She continues, "I wanted to follow slower so I could watch the man and look for any others. I'd rather get caught than them find you three." She glances at each of us, and we share a knowing look. Laura has always been the protector, being the oldest, and has taken all the risks to keep us safe.

Luna acknowledges, "We'd have died if it wasn't for you, Laura." The three of us nod, knowing it's the truth. She was brave when we were kids, and it followed her as she got older. She was the one who taught me how to swim and catch fish as well as face down anything we were uncertain of. She made sure we learned how to survive, and without her, none of us would be here right now.

"I did what any oldest in the family would do, even if we were somewhat new to each other. Plus, I knew Mom would tan my hide if I didn't come back with you all." She plays it off, making their adoptive mother smile.

"So you live with Hunter now?" Luna asks, moving the conversation away from the heavy, and I nod.

"You love him?" Mary's next to pipe up.

"Yes, he saved me. Something happened when I went back to the hut, and I didn't end up making it all the way there."

Hunter leans forward, giving my thigh a reassuring squeeze.

"We think you had a serious allergic reaction. By the time we found you, you were barely breathing."

"Oh my God," Mary gasps, her hand moving to her mouth.

"Hey, I'm right here and better than ever."

Laura nods. "I heard a loud noise and saw your group coming toward our spot. I thought Aura was already safe somewhere, so I gathered Mary and Luna, and we ran. I was too scared to stay longer and see what your group wanted."

Now it's my turn to gape. "The entire time you were right there, you saw them… you guys could've come home with me."

Hunter offers me a tender look. "No, beautiful, she did the right thing. She kept herself safe, which was the smartest thing to do. I wish I'd known I'd find you there, I'd have come better prepared for others, and maybe circumstances would've been different."

Their mother stands. "What matters to me most is you're all here and safe now. We've each been given a second chance at life, and I don't ever intend to waste it. Now, who's ready for a slice of cake? I have a delicious strawberry cream cake waiting on the counter to be sliced up and shared."

I smile gratefully and stand, then with a burst of emotion, I hug her. "Thank you for loving and adopting such amazing daughters. They were everything to me on the island and will be a big piece of my heart for the rest of my life. You should be very proud of everything they've done."

"Oh, honey…" she pats my back, "… I'm extremely proud of all of you. You're the strongest young women I know."

We follow her into the kitchen, and I'm ambushed by my friends. "We're not going anywhere," Laura chides.

"Yeah, you're stuck with us," Luna offers with a flirty wink.

Mary lightly tugs on a fallen strand of my hair. "We love you too much, you're one of us. We've adopted you into our family, too, if you haven't caught on. We've spent too many years with you to let you off the hook now."

I smile widely, used to her teasing me in the past about how I was meant to be adopted with them. She used to say it's why I ended up with them looking out for me. It was meant to be.

"Love you, too, Mary."

She smiles and presses a sweet kiss on my cheek. "Hunter, has she sung for you yet? Our Aura has quite the voice."

He smirks. He hears me daily. "Yes, but not for me, only our plants."

We all laugh, and I can't deny it because it's true.

"We need to bring you to karaoke," Luna suggests, causing snickers to erupt between them.

"What is it?" I ask.

Hunter leans in, chuckling and shares, "You sing in front of people to random songs you choose. It's usually horrible, anyone can do it, and there's a lot of screeching by the end of the night."

I giggle, and Mary nods, grinning ear to ear. "He's right. We found a place down the street the other night and sang our hearts out. We had a blast."

The five of them laugh, and I find myself beaming. This is how it was always meant to be—me with my three friends and Hunter by my side. I never knew something was wrong until I got back home and realized my world was messy, full of heartache and hunger. However, now everything makes sense, and we can all have our happily ever after.

EPILOGUE I

HUNTER

One Year Later...

Aura climbs off my bike, and as soon as I join her, she says, "Let's do it."

"Do what, beautiful?"

"Get married." Her hair's windblown as usual, and her cheeks are kissed by the sun. Her looking like this has me wanting to say yes to anything she asks for. In most cases, I do, but I won't budge on our wedding. We've been through this already.

"I love you. I want to say yes, but it's going to be a hard no." We just came back from Luna's wedding, and it has my woman itching for the opportunity to jet off and elope. "You've put far too much into making sure our wedding is everything you've dreamed of. I know you want the whole shebang, so we're going to do this right and stick to the plan. Once the big 'I do' is over, we can fly to Vegas or wherever your heart desires to get married a million times over. It'll happen, and I promise you there's nothing I want more than my ring on your finger."

She pouts. The brat knows what that bottom lip does to my willpower. The pang in my chest hits me, telling me to give in, but I fight it.

"I want to marry you now. I'm ready."

I nod. "I am, too, but it still doesn't change things. Our wedding is in a week, and we can wait seven days. I have a fantastic idea for the meantime, though."

"Oh yeah?" She grins, instantly intrigued as we walk into her parents' house. "Tell me, handsome."

"When we get back home, you can put on your fluffy dress 'cause, let's be honest, I know you picked something fluffy," I begin, and she nods, egging me on. I bet it's sparkly too. She'll be blinged out for our special day and look like a true princess. "I'll see you wrapped up in the gorgeous monstrosity tonight, and we can go over our vows. Then, last but definitely not least, I'll rip the dress off your sexy body like I plan to, and we can have crazy exciting wedding sex."

"Hunter!" She gapes, and her mom interrupts.

"You're not ripping the wedding dress. I suggest you find a knock-off if you want to go caveman."

Aura turns bright red while I chuckle, entertained by her response. "I'm down for that option as well. You wouldn't happen to have one we can borrow, Lucia, do you?"

She scowls but ends up laughing and shaking her head. "You're practically my son, Hunter, and she's my only daughter. Let's keep the sex talk to a minimum. I don't want any of it venturing into my mind. I'll send her father to interrupt you all night on your wedding."

I shrug, not perturbed in the slightest. "If you insist, but it'd bring our conversations up a notch," I joke, and Aura smacks me in my gut. "Easy, woman, it was just a suggestion. Besides, I'm pretty sure you were going to agree to my idea until your mom overheard."

She sends me a mock glare, glancing from her mother's back to me as we follow her to the dining room for dinner. "I most certainly was not."

I send her a wink because she's bluffing, and she's adorable. I know my woman, and she loves the crazy shit we do. "So, if I show up with a wedding dress..." I trail off. Her mom sends me a look over her shoulder, and Aura puts her finger over her mouth, trying to shush me. "Maybe I'll ask your dad, I'm sure he'd enjoy the idea."

Aura shoves me, making me chuckle louder. She's playful, and I love every minute of it. She knows how to take my teasing and usually gives it right back to me. All in all, I've never been happier in my life. Finding her was the best thing to ever happen to me. Marrying her will be the next, there's not a doubt in my mind.

"Philip," Steven greets me with a handshake and then hugs his daughter. He still calls me by my given name as does Lucia, but it doesn't irk me, considering everyone outside my club brothers and Aura use it.

My parents soon join us, and we all exchange pleasantries with them as well, eventually making our way to the dining table for dinner. We lucked out and didn't get stuck with reception activities since Luna's new husband whisked her off on their honeymoon right after the ceremony.

"You look stunning as always, Aura," my mom says as we scoot our heavy, expertly carved chairs in. The staff brings out our dinner salads and fills our wine glasses. "You're going to make such a gorgeous bride."

Wedding talk has been everything for the past six months, and I'm tired of the same repeated conversations. I don't say as much because Aura eats it up, and her happiness is everything to me. I swore to myself when I was rotting downstairs that I'd get out of there and make sure I kept the smile on my woman's face.

"Thank you, I was attempting to talk your son into a quicker wedding earlier, but he wasn't having it," she tattles.

Both our mothers chime in simultaneously, begging her not to change the date. Everything's in place, and we all want her to have the wedding of her dreams, especially after being stuck on the island for so long and having nothing. She deserves to have it all and more.

Steven clears his throat. "I asked you all here today to discuss the future of our company. We believe it's time for some changes." Everyone quiets at once, turning our attention to the man sitting at the head of the table. He glances at each of us, saying, "Lucia and I dreamed of having our daughter take over Beautiful Botanicals one day. With her kidnapping and disappearance for so many years, we never thought it would be a possibility." He draws in a breath, becoming emotional over the mention of her abduction. I think it all hits us straight in the chest whenever it's brought up. We know damn well we need to discuss it, but none of us want to remember it.

Lucia reaches for Aura's hand as her father continues, "We're getting older and would like to take a further step back from the company if possible. We have people in place to run it, but we still need one of us to oversee everything, to keep it steered in the right direction. We have a core set of values and treasured employees we want to remain with the company."

"Just ask them, honey," Lucia coaxes, flashing him a tender smile.

Steven's stare bounces from me to Aura and back. "Aura, we'd like you to step on board if you feel comfortable enough. Your presence and influence would be a great honor for us."

Lucia nods, "Yes, we love you, dear. You have the gift of a green thumb and fresh ideas. We're tired."

Aura bites her lip, looking as if her shoulders weigh a thousand pounds. "I'd love to, truly. However, we're all aware I have a major disadvantage holding me back."

My mother asks, "What are you talking about, Aura?"

"I can't read. I've learned a few things, but I can't read a full sentence without struggling. How on earth can I ever possibly run a company if I can't even read the names of the plants?" Her lower lip trembles, and I reach for her other hand, squeezing it to offer her my silent support if she needs it right now. She's strong, but I never want her to feel as if she's struggling with something alone.

Steven takes a drink of his wine and further explains, "We've considered the possibility of you bringing your reading up tonight, and we believe we've found a solution. If Hunter is willing, you'll be named CEO, and he'll be offered the CAO/CIO position."

I lean in, quietly explaining, "You would be the top-tier boss as Chief Executive Officer overseeing everything. I'd be the Chief Administrative Officer and Chief Information Officer. They look after the company's administrative management as well as establish and maintain a strategy for protecting company information and data." I was offered something similar for my dad's company before he sold it.

Steven nods, peering my way. "Exactly. This will put you in front of the paperwork while Aura has a chance to develop and strengthen her reading skills."

"I still feel underqualified," she murmurs.

Lucia cuts in as she does anytime Aura begins to doubt herself. "The benefit of owning the company is we can hire or appoint anyone we see fit. Your father and I will work closely with you both to groom you to take over… we won't leave you high and dry. We want our legacy to continue through you and become yours as well as whatever you set your heart on. Perhaps one day it'll be passed on to grandchildren."

Aura glances at me, shooting me a look. I can read it being around her so much. I know she wants my input, but I'm just as confused as to what the right answer would be for either of us.

"Hunter has his own business, he's a bounty hunter. He loves his work, and he tells me all the time how much fun he has chasing after people with his brothers."

My dad finally breaks his silence. "While I was hoping Philip would take up my line of work, I respect his decision to walk his own path. He's worked damn hard to build what he has. This doesn't seem fair of you to ask for so much from him, Steven."

Aura's father agrees. "I know it's a heavy responsibility to request of him, Henry, but without them, we'll have to begin incorporating shareholders and a board of directors. I don't want to go that route, but I will if the kids don't want Beautiful Botanicals."

Throwing away my soon-to-be wife's future company seems careless to do it with a simple yes or no. I don't want to be the one to make the call and regret it in the future. The thought doesn't sit right, especially since the only real reason she's turning it down is because of her reading. We've been working on the basics, but we could hire someone to truly help teach her what she needs to learn in-depth. Her mother and father promise to teach her the company's ways, so the only obstacle left is my business and my brothers. I can be a part of the club for the rest of my life no matter what I do for a living, but I won't take away my brothers' means of legal income. What kind of man, friend, brother, or boss would I be if I let them go without securing something for them first?

"If I agree to do my part, I have one concession."

"Name it," Steven responds, always ready to do business and negotiate.

"I need my own set of offices and equipment at the headquarters for my brothers. I can help Aura with the Botanical empire while running my business as well."

"But your trips," Aura interrupts. "You love your work, Hunter."

I nod. "I do, and I'll never be a three-piece-suit Wall Street type of guy, but I can do this. My brothers can take on the jobs they want, and I'll help where needed. I can bounce between your company and mine in the same office. As long as everyone understands I won't be in the office every day, and I may need to leave for days at a time." I look toward Steven and Lucia. "I can be the backup Aura needs. I won't take this opportunity from her if this is something she wants. It has to be her decision, though, no pressure. And I'm wearing my jeans, not those prissy-ass dress pants."

My parents shoot me with a look. They used to tell me to cool it with my mouth, but they've learned I don't listen. I do what I want when I want, and if they push me, I'll only resist more. Still, not wanting to be disrespectful, I mutter a quick apology for cursing at the dinner table.

Aura leans in, tugging my scruffy chin toward her until I turn, so she can press a kiss to my lips. It's short and sweet. She leans her forehead against mine and murmurs, "I love you so much. Thank you for doing this."

"I'll always be there for you whether it's to rescue you, read you a story, or help you run a company. I'm all in, and I love you too."

She smiles widely and turns back to our parents. "We'll do it."

I lean in, whispering my plans for when we get home, "I'm going to fuck you so hard for this, I hope you know."

With a devilish grin, she says, "Promises, promises. I'll hold you to it."

It looks like we're running a company together, but I wouldn't want to do it with anyone else. She's my everything, and I intend to give her the life she's always deserved, filled with happiness and hot-as-sin nights.

EPILOGUE II

AURA

Ten Years Later...

One of the most difficult obstacles to overcome in my life has been my inability to read. While on the island for so many years, I never needed to know how. I learned to write my name from the others, but otherwise, there wasn't ever any writing involved. Sure, we doodled and made up different stories for the pictures, but it was never the same thing. When I returned home and realized how vital it is to succeed, I was overwhelmed and embarrassed.

Thanks to persistent parents and a caring husband, I've overcome my lack of reading and writing skills. I didn't stop there, and learning became a passion for me. I kept taking class after class to help me write and understand things better, and I couldn't get enough. I'm grateful for my persistence as I sit here reading the series of short stories Mary wrote for my baby.

They all have their own families now, who I love like an extension of my own. Laura and her wife just adopted an adorable set of twin babies. Their family had been visiting from the

Philippines when there was a horrendous accident. It killed the twins' birth parents, and when Child Protective Services discovered there wasn't any other living family, Laura and her wife hired an amazing lawyer who helped them fight to adopt the babies.

    Luna followed her passion for singing. It took her to Nashville, where she met a country music star in some hole-in-the-wall dive bar. They fell hopelessly in love and have a beautiful home in Tennessee. She just had their third baby and released her fourth album. They have an in-home studio where her husband helps to produce her music. They sang a duet Christmas album that I drove Hunter crazy with. It's on repeat each year from November through the end of December, and I can't seem to get enough of it. We visit them occasionally, but it's still hard having her so far away. I usually pop on her music when I start to miss her, and it makes me feel like she's in the room, singing to me like she used to.

    Mary stayed close to home, moving in the same neighborhood as her adopted mom. She and her husband have one child together, a cute little boy who's borderline genius. We get all the invites for his school functions and birthdays, and we always do our best to go and show our support. Mary discovered her love for telling stories wasn't only a hobby but also her career. She's published several children's and adult books. I'm proud to say I have copies of them all. I have personally signed copies at home as well as a set for the office in case anyone wants to read them. I like to think her amazing stories helped spur on my love for reading as I continue to devour any book she throws my way.

    My parents are doing great, retired, living their best life, and over the moon with excitement to have a new grandchild. They threw us a huge party to celebrate last week. It was quite entertaining to see several of Hunter's brothers clad in their leather jackets with their families, mixed in with my parents' stuffy friends and people from work. I've gotten used to everyone, as most are around often and in passing at work, but it's still interesting to see how everyone stands out so differently from one another.

It reminded me of our wedding several years ago when Hunter insisted on wearing his leather jacket to get married in. His groomsmen, who are also his MC brothers, were all dressed the same way. On my side of the aisle, it looked like we stepped out of a fairy tale in puffy, elaborate gowns. It certainly made for some great wedding photos, which, of course, I've hung all around our home.

As for Diana and her murderous plot against me, my father went on a massive tirade after everything happened. He demanded we find anyone associated with his psychopathic sister's plan and make them pay for the lives they've altered. Hunter and his MC brothers were front and center in the investigation, and with the help of the state police, were able to turn over new evidence.

Having my friends and their mother around helped to fill in some missing pieces from their angle. My dad handed over everything Diana had for investigating, and Hunter broke into her laptop and accessed her hard drive. Once he copied it all, they went to the police so they could step in and do their own digging. While I'm sure my husband would've preferred making everyone involved disappear forever, it wasn't the right way to do things. He toes the line of good and bad at times, but somehow, I always manage to get him back where he needs to be with his conscience.

The police were able to implicate a gang cell and put them all behind bars for their involvement. I'm sure Hunter made a few magically disappear, but the rest were allowed to serve time for their crimes. It was wonderful to get a sense of closure with that part of our life, but it also dredged up so many intense feelings I wasn't expecting. It took some time, but we managed to work through them together.

Hunter and I have been married for ten years now, and while

some may think it's a long time to be together before having children, we took the path best for us. My father did as he said, and eventually, he fully handed over Beautiful Botanicals to me. With Hunter's help, we struggled at first, but eventually caught the hang of things. I discovered I love working at my family company and threw myself in headfirst. It's one of the reasons why we've waited to have children. I wanted to be successful in my own right and live a little, as my mother likes to say. I can honestly say I never pictured my life as the CEO of a large company, but it's fulfilled me in ways I didn't know I needed.

Hunter and I have traveled the world together, exploring everything and building our relationship. He's been the love of my life and my best friend. Now when I think of things, I couldn't imagine my life turning out any other way than it has.

It's scary to look back now, knowing I would've died if it weren't for him accidentally finding me. He truly has been my knight in shining armor, and it's only fitting he's in the VII Knights MC.

Thank you for reading *Hunter*.
I hope you enjoyed the story and will consider leaving a positive review if you did.
– Sapphire

THE END

Hunter

ALSO BY SAPPHIRE

Oath Keepers MC Series
Exposed
Relinquish
Forsaken Control
Friction
Sweet Surrender – free short story in Newsletter

Oath Keepers MC Hybrid Series
Princess
Love and Obey – free short story in Newsletter
Daydream
Baby
Chevelle
Cherry
Heathen
Hollywood

Russkaya Mafiya Series
Secrets
Corrupted
Corrupted Counterparts – free short story in Newsletter

Sapphire Knight

Unwanted Sacrifices
Undercover Intentions

Dirty Down South Series
Freight Train
3 Times the Heat
Bliss

The Vendetti Famiglia
The Vendetti Empire - Part 1
The Vendetti Queen - Part 2
The Vendetti Seven – Part 3
The Vendetti Coward – Part 4
The Vendetti Devil – Part 5 (coming soon)

Harvard Academy Elite
Little White Lies
Ugly Dark Truth

Royal Bastards MC Texas
Opposites Attract/Bastard

Kings of Carnage MC Series
Bash – Vice President
Sterling - Prospect

The Chicago Crew
Gangster
Mad Max

VII Knights MC
Hunter – Nomad

Hunter

Complete Standalones
Gangster
Unexpected Forfeit
The Main Event – free short story in Newsletter
Oath Keepers MC Collection
Russian Roulette
Tease – Short Story Collection
Oath Keepers MC Hybrid Collection
Vendetti Duet
Harvard Academy Elite
Viking – free newsletter short story in Newsletter
Dirty Down South Collection

STRAWBERRY CREAM CAKE

Cake Ingredients:

1/2 cup butter
1-1/2 cups all-purpose flour
2 teaspoons baking powder
1/2 teaspoon salt
1/2 cup sugar
3 large eggs
1/2 teaspoon vanilla extract
1/2 cup milk
Filling Ingredients:
1 pound strawberries - sliced
1/2 cup sugar
1 teaspoon unflavored gelatin
1-1/2 cups heavy cream

Hunter

Directions:

Preheat oven to 350 degrees. Butter or spray an 8-inch cake pan.

Whisk together flour, baking powder, and salt.

In a separate bowl, mix butter and 1/2 cup sugar until light and fluffy. Add eggs and vanilla, mix after each. Add in milk and flour, mixing until smooth.

Bake 30 to 35 minutes and let cool. Cut cake in the middle to layer filling between the two.

For filling and topping: In a large bowl, mix the strawberries and 1/4 cup sugar.

Use 2 tablespoons cold water in a saucepan, add gelatin, let soften for 5 minutes. Place saucepan over low heat, and whisk until gelatin is dissolved, then let cool.

Mix cream and remaining sugar in a large bowl until soft peaks form. Add gelatin mixture and mix until peaks form.

Split half of the strawberries and whipped cream and spread over the bottom layer, then use the remaining over the top cake layer. Refrigerate for a minimum of one hour.

ACKNOWLEDGMENTS

My husband—I love you, and I'm thankful for you.

My boys—You're my whole world. I love you both, this never changes. I can't express how grateful I am for your support and belief in me. You're quick to tell me that my career makes you proud and that I make you proud. As far as Mom wins go, that one takes the cake, even if I do send 'mom memes.' I love you with every beat of my heart, and I will forever.

My Dogs—You guys are assholes, but I love you so much it makes my heart ache. Please stop barking and chugging water when I'm trying to write.

Women that inspire—Hilary Storm, Lindsey King, and Victoria Ashley. I love you, ladies! Thank you for always being there, even when I'm a shitty friend and never text first. You mean so much to me.

PA—Paige, you've stepped in and made my life easier. I appreciate and value your time. The fact that you're a Virgo with purple hair also kinda makes me think it was fate we met!

Editor—Swish Editing & Design. Your hard work makes mine stand out, and I'm so grateful! Thank you for pouring hours into my passion and being kind to me. Thank you for your support, especially on such short notice.

Tall Story—Thank you for designing this cover. The thorns were an awesome addition I never imagined, and I value your professionalism.

Photographer, Wander Aguiar, and model, Zack Salaun—Thank you for allowing me to have your art on my cover, it's stunning. Your talent knows no end. And Zack, I liked your images so much, I got two :) Thank you for encompassing my rough bikers so well!

My Blogger, Bookstagrammer, and TikTok Friends—YOU ARE AMAZING! You take a new chance on me with each book and, in return, share my passion with the world. You never truly get enough credit, and I'm forever grateful for every share and shout-out.

My Readers—I love you. You make my life possible, so thank you. I can't wait to meet many of you this year and in the future. To those of you leaving me the awesome spoiler-free reviews, you motivate me to keep writing. For that, I'll forever be grateful as this is my passion in life.

And as always, ADOPT DON'T SHOP! Save a life today and adopt from a rescue or your local animal shelter.
#ProudDobermanMom #LastHopeDobermanRescue

CONNECT WITH ME ONLINE

Stay up to date with
Wall Street Journal and USA Today Bestselling Author
Sapphire Knight

WEBSITE
http://www.authorsapphireknight.com/

BOOKBUB
http://bit.ly/bookbubSK

TWITTER
http://bit.ly/tweetSK

AMAZON
http://bit.ly/SKzon

INSTAGRAM
http://bit.ly/SKinstag

NEWSLETTER
http://bit.ly/SKnightNewsletter

FACEBOOK
http://bit.ly/SKfb

TIKTOK
http://bit.ly/SKTik

PINTEREST
http://bit.ly/pinmeSK

ABOUT THE AUTHOR

Sapphire Knight is a *Wall Street Journal* and *USA Today* Bestselling author with many books published that reflect what she loves to read herself.

Sapphire's a Texas girl who's crazy about football. She's always had a passion for writing. She originally studied psychology and feels that it's added to her drive in writing.

Sapphire is the proud mom of two handsome boys. She's been married to the love of her life, an Army veteran, for seventeen years. When she's not busy in her writing cave, she's playing with her three Doberman Pinschers. She loves to donate to help animals and watch a good action movie.

http://www.authorsapphireknight.com
and also find her on Bookbub!

Printed in Great Britain
by Amazon